SOUL OF A VAMPIRE

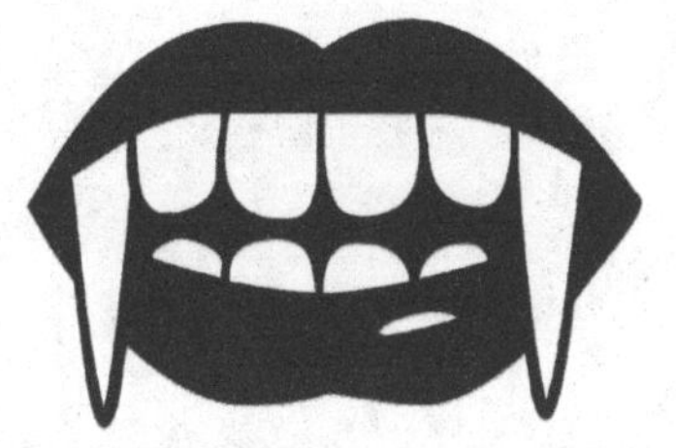

SOUL OF A VAMPIRE

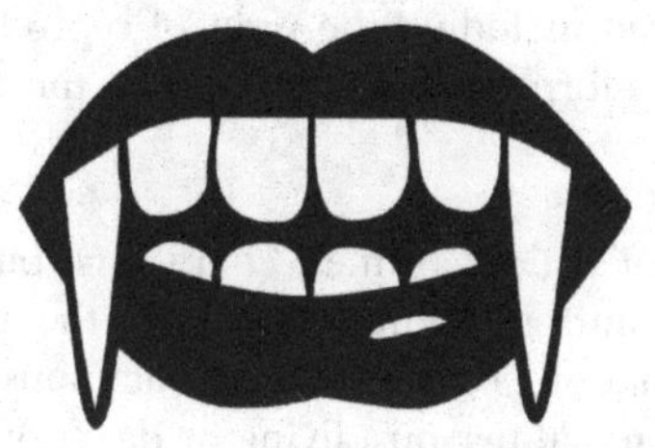

SILENCIO MARQUEZ

EST.   2019
BLKDOG

PROLOGUE

Zeke was out that night at a bar near his apartment building in Calgary, Alberta Canada. It was early spring, and the air still had a nip in it. He could clearly see the breath of others as they passed by. The air was filled with the scent of roses and tulips and flowering dogwood. The place he was heading to wasn't fancy. A hole in the wall that was dark and smelled like cigarette smoke from the days when you could still smoke inside. There were a variety of other smells, few of them pleasant. There was the smell of alcohol that was nearly overwhelming and the restroom in the back that smelled like old, stale piss, and the smell of humans and the delectable blood running through their veins. That was what he was there for. Zeke could get drunk, could outdrink anyone in that place, but that wasn't his goal. There was once that he and his ex, Kris went out drinking after a particularly taxing night searching for willing victims when they were still terrorizing London. They nearly drank the place dry, and Zeke left Kris in his dust after a couple of hours. Vampires didn't have to worry about their livers. Only blood mattered. He was there to find a willing victim on which to feed. That which all vampires sought when they went out at night.

He went up to the bar. The woman standing behind it gave him a little grin. She wanted to be somewhere else. Zeke could tell from the look on her face. The look that said, "I hate this job and this place and your face, but I have to do it." Zeke could appreciate that. Over seven hundred years he's had a lot of jobs he hated. He smiled back at her. She was a tall woman with shoulder-length, red hair. Lovely, but she was not what he was looking for. She was a woman you took home and made love to, but her blood smelled like armpit.

"What can I get for you?" She asked him disinterestedly.

"Ah, Whiskey, I think."

"Really? You're a whiskey man?"

"Tonight I am. I've had just about everything over the years," Zeke replied, "I don't drink very often, but sometimes you just feel the urge."

"What kind do you want?"

"The Irishman," Zeke leaned against the bar heavily.

"That's expensive stuff."

"Of course, it's expensive, love. Most things are these days."

"Love, eh?" She seemed a little surprised.

"Sorry," he replied, "I'm a bit worried tonight. Family trouble has my mind twisted."

"Well, then, we'd better get you what you need."

"Thank you," he replied.

She got him his drink. It was expensive, but he paid gladly. She left him then and tended the other people at the bar. He stood there and sipped his drink. He didn't want a chair. Zeke wasn't in the mood to sit and drink. He wanted to stand there and smell everything. He loved the scent of people. They all smelled different. Some were sweet, some were salty, but they all had one thing in common. They were all food. Zeke was on the hunt, and places like this were like a buffet.

The vampire sniffed the air, parsing the scents that floated by him. A particularly sweet scent wafting on the air made him salivate in hunger. His breath quivered with anticipation. A young man who was going to be sweeter than candy if Zeke could talk him into playing. Vampires couldn't feed on unwilling humans. It was against the law. However, if he could talk the man into it he was in for a lovely night.

Zeke turned and looked around, attempting to find the source of the scent in the dark room. There he was, a young man with long, dark curls and emerald eyes. Beautiful, just as Zeke had suspected. The beautiful ones always smelled the sweetest. Zeke caught his eye and gave him an alluring smile. The man beckoned him to his table. Zeke reached behind him and grabbed his glass. He hadn't finished yet. He swirled the last of the amber liquid in his glass. He sipped the last of it and then left the glass on the bar.

Zeke went over to the man's table. Sat down across from him. Zeke hadn't ordered another drink, he had something far more interesting in front of him now. His new companion noticed. "You're not having anything?"

"Oh, not right now. Everything in moderation. What about you? Can I buy you a drink?"

The young man laughed, "Sure. What were you having before? Maybe we can both have the same?"

"Whiskey. It's not everyday stuff, but when you drink as rarely as I do it's alright to splurge a bit. Hold on a second and I'll take care of it."

Zeke went back to the bar and got two more of the whiskeys. Expensive, but necessary. He went back to the table and sat across from the man, handing him the drink. His new friend tried to give him money to pay for it. "Don't worry about it," Zeke said, "It's all good. So, what's your name?"

"My name's Andrew," he fidgeted with the zipper on his jacket.

"Andrew," Zeke mulled it over, "that's a nice name. My name is Zeke."

"Now that's unique."

"Not really," Zeke sipped his drink. "It's short for Ezekiel. My parents loved that name."

"Jewish, isn't it?"

"Yes, it is," Zeke replied. "Though I haven't really considered myself Jewish in a long time."

"Really? I didn't know that was a thing. I thought Jewish people were always Jewish."

"The situation with my family is complicated," Zeke leaned back in his chair and smiled, "most of them are dead."

"I'm sorry to hear that," Andrew furrowed his brow.

Zeke felt it best to reassure him, "We were never close, me and the family. I still have my sister though."

"Well, that's good I suppose," he replied.

"And what about you?" Zeke mused, "what's your story, Andrew?"

The young man sipped his drink. He smelled so good. Like chocolate cake or warm bread. Simply delectable. "Not much to tell. I came up here to see friends. Decided to spend an extra night just to check out the city."

"Where did you come from?"

"Oh, I came from Seattle. Most of my family lives there, but most of my friends live here. It's nice enough."

"Yes, I suppose."

Andrew finished his drink and gave Zeke a smile. "Well, I'd better be going."

Zeke looked into Andrew's eyes and knew what he saw there. The man had assessed him and found him to be unworthy. "I see," he said. That was when the first flash of pain came to him. Flaring through his head like a hot nail. "Yes, perhaps that's best."

"Thanks for the drink."

"No problem. It's always good to meet new people," He winced as the pain hit him again. Zeke got up from the table. He stumbled away from the table. People probably thought he was drunk, but vampires didn't get drunk easily. He felt like he was going to vomit. He didn't know what was happening to him. He made it to the back door and stumbled out into the darkened alley.

He vomited blood everywhere in the alley as he fell to his knees. What the hell was happening to him? There was someone standing in front of him. A woman in a red dress. He tried to look up at her. Zeke was sure he knew who it was. Then he heard her voice and he knew.

"Hello, Zeke," the voice belonged to his sister.

He fell onto his side. The pavement was rough and gritty. It was wet with something. Given all the smells that were in the alley like piss and vomit and, amazingly blood, he didn't want to even guess what it was. "Anna, what have you done to me?"

"It's not important," he heard her say.

"Are you going to kill me now, sister?"

"I'm not going to kill you, no. But there will be death," she replied, pacing around him in her high heels. "There have been so many deaths lately. All because people can't stay out of vampire business."

"This is about Charles, isn't it?" It was, but he wasn't tracking very well.

"Good lord," she kicked him in the gut, "of course it's about Charles. You got into his business. He wanted to kill you, but I told him I would take care of it. Vampires are at the top of the food chain, my dear brother. Charles is trying to recreate the world as it should be."

"You're going to do this through murder?"

"Oh yes, brother. I warned you to stay out of the way, but you wouldn't listen, Now, you have to be dealt with."

"You are going to kill me," He was losing consciousness. His head was spinning wildly, and his eyes could barely focus on what was in front of him.

"Don't worry, Zeke," Anna said, "When you wake up everything will be fine. You'll see."

He didn't have time to wonder what she meant. He closed his eyes and that was all.

***

When Zeke awoke, he was lying on the floor of his apartment covered in blood. Blood that had been sweet when it still flowed through a man's veins. It was everywhere and in the middle of the room, a body was sprawled on the floor. A dead body. A young man in a brown leather jacket that he couldn't remember. His throat had been both bitten and slashed. He had bled out onto the floor. His vampire's eyes could see well enough in the dark. One of the benefits of being a nocturnal creature. Right now, he wished he couldn't.

Zeke couldn't remember who he was or what had happened. All he could do was hope that he wasn't responsible. Had he killed this person? Why did his head hurt so badly? Had he murdered someone in a rage? Zeke wasn't a raging sort of person, but something happened last night, and he didn't know what. He looked closely at the young man's face, but he couldn't put a name to it. He needed help.

The first name that came to mind was that of Kristof Kellman who worked as a detective at the Calgary division of the Magical Laws Division, a crime-fighting force that solved crimes on behalf of the supernatural community. Zeke got shakily to his feet and stumbled to the door. He had to get to Kris. He was an old friend. He would help. Or at least, he hoped he would. Zeke reached into his pocket to see if he still had his phone. It was gone. Anna must have taken it so that he couldn't call for help. He hoped, beyond hope, that Kris could save him, even if he didn't deserve it.

CHAPTER 1

Kristof Kellmen didn't really like people. That meant anything that could pass as human including supernatural creatures like vampires, werewolves, and dragons. Everyone lied, which just seemed to be the way people worked. Still, it was frustrating when it got in the way of his job as an investigator for the Magical Law Division. Even among magical creatures, there were crimes. It was his job to make sure the criminals, no matter who they were, faced justice.

Kris loved his job and did it well. People were the piece of it that made it messy. Especially one night when his former lover, Ezekiel Yonah, showed up at his door covered in blood and looking the most distressed he had ever looked in his life. Kris didn't know what to make of it at first. Zeke was a vampire, as was Kris. Being covered in blood wasn't completely out of place for either of them. It was the distress that was out of place.

"What the hell happened to you?" Kris asked, somewhat miffed that Zeke was bothering him with what was probably nonsense.

"I messed up," Zeke said with tears in his eyes, "I didn't mean to kill him, but somehow I did. I don't even remember taking him home with me. When I came to, there he was on my floor, dead as a door-nail. I really fucked up bad."

"If someone is dead, yeah, I would say you fucked up pretty bad. Come in and tell me about it."

Zeke stepped into Kris's apartment. It was a small place in the Hillhurst community of Calgary, Alberta, Canada. It was a nice neighborhood. There were tall red maples with large fluttering leaves that danced in the light, spring breeze. The trees were a bit sparse this time of year, but they smelled like the earth and recent rain. It was a fresh, beautiful place. The building he lived in was a two-story building with a brick facade and large windows and a large red door. It was the kind of place the felt like a home, even if you weren't the kind of person who believed in a home. Kris felt grounded here for the first time in many years.

While the sun wouldn't make Kris go up in a burst of flames, it did tire him out. Blood was a necessary part of a vampire's diet, some could eat other foods and quite enjoyed them. He was one of those vampires. When the doorbell had rung, Kris was about to sit down and have a beer while munching on dark chocolates dipped in blood sauce. He had a thing for type AB- that he thought paired really nicely with chocolate and booze.

Sadly, Zeke had gotten in the way of his good time. The vampire was distraught as Kris led him into the living room. Zeke wanted to sit, but Kris stopped him, "wait for a second, will you? I'm going to go find a sheet or something to put down. You're covered in blood, and I don't want it all over my tan sofa. Far easier to replace a sheet than a sofa."

"Whatever," Zeke said. Kris went into the bedroom and began to look in his closet for a clean sheet. He finally found one. It was wedged under a pile of sweaters. He yanked on it. The sweaters fell on his head. He stood there for a moment, sheet in hand in a pile of sweaters.

"Lovely," he said to himself as he stepped out of them. He took the sheet back into the living room where he found Zeke still standing where he had left him, a worried expression on his face. His eyes were staring into a void that seemed to exist in the cracks between the slats of the wood floor. Kris walked past him and began to spread the sheet out on the sofa. Once he had it how he wanted it, he said, "come sit and tell me about it. Start at the beginning. Anything you can remember. This is where I play good cop and you tell me everything you remember, whether you think it matters or not. Everything matters. Then we'll check out the crime scene and I'll act like a bad cop and try to save you from yourself if I have to. I'll probably regret it, but it's not the first thing I'll have regretted given our past." Zeke had come to him as a friend. It was probably best to let it start out like that.

Zeke walked over, his eyes wide and staring in dazed confusion. Whatever happened it had really shaken him. He sat down carefully on the sofa, Kris sat across from him in his La-z-boy. It was a recliner, he wasn't going to sit back. However, he was going to eat his chocolates while he listened. "Go ahead," he said as he picked up the cup of blood and the wedge of chocolate and dipped it. He put it into his mouth he savored the flavors as Zeke began his story.

"I was out last night like I go out almost every Friday. There's this bar that I like to frequent. A place where humans and vamps like to mingle. There was this guy, and he was so nice and chatty and everything. We talked, and then I started not to feel so well, so I left. I didn't even leave with him. The last thing I remember is stepping out onto the sidewalk outside the bar, and then...nothing. When I woke up, I was at my place and he was there too, and he was dead. He wasn't even completely drained. He bled out all over my floor."

"He bled out?" Kris said, "were there any bites on him at all?"

"He was bitten once on the neck, and he was also slashed," Zeke said.

"And you had nothing to do with slashing him?"

"If I did, I don't remember. I don't even remember how I got home."

"That's interesting. Well, you're a vampire. It takes forever for vampires to get drunk. So, there's little chance that getting drunk made you pass out. Then again, I've seen you drunk. I know how you can get."

"Well, maybe there was something in my drink?"

"Like what?" Kris asked, "It's not like you can drug a vamp like a human either." Then a thought came to him, "there are some substances that can act like drugs to vamps, though. Was whatever you were drinking unattended at any time?"

"Maybe I turned my back on it once or twice. I get distracted easily. But you know me, I can't resist a hot chatty guy," Zeke gave Kris a sly smile.

Kris rolled his eyes, "may I remind you that you cheated on me?" He continued to munch on his chocolate dipped in blood. This was good stuff. "You're lucky that I'm helping you at all."

"I know. I'm sorry..."

"I'll need to test your blood," Kris said, "to see if it's been tainted by anything."

"What do you think it might be? I know you suspect something that you're not telling me."

"Just let me finish my chocolate and then I will test you and we'll see if you've been dosed with dead man's blood."

"Dead man's blood?" Zeke had that look on his face like he couldn't believe what he was saying, "How could something like this happen?"

"More easily than you might think. Both vampires and people who are around them know that it affects us. I suspect that might be the culprit. I think someone set you up for murder."

"Set up? Why? Who would do that?"

"That's the question. And I'm going to try and find an answer for you," Kris continued to munch on his chocolate, "which I shall get to after chocolate time. Maybe you should go take a shower before we head over to your place. It's difficult to be inconspicuous when you're covered in blood."

This is not something he would usually do. Something told him that this was more than a simple murder. If this had anything to do with the vampire leadership he would have to try and keep the MLD out of it. Leadership didn't like it when law enforcement got involved with things that were considered vampire affairs. Kris often found himself stuck in the middle of this debate and didn't like picking sides. He couldn't believe this was happening on his day off. It was even more painful than it was Zeke. No one interfered with his chocolate time. Not even a very old friend who needed his help.

CHAPTER 2

Kris stood with Zeke in his bathroom and he bit into Zeke's arm. Zeke cried out, but Kris held his arm tight. He sucked on the other vampire's blood for a moment. He dropped Zeke's arm, "I can taste it. It's disgusting Dead man's blood," he said. He glared at Zeke. The crap in Zeke's blood had muddied his chocolate daze. "You're a pain in my arse," he said to Zeke, "we should go to your place and see what the damage is."

Zeke's place not far from where Kris lived. That was another thing that bothered Kris. The fact that he had to avoid his ex. Kris didn't like people very much as it was. When he looked at himself in the mirror, he didn't exactly see a catch there. He was short, had silvery hair, and never felt that he was what others would consider handsome. An assessment that seemed to be accurate given his state of always being alone.

Zeke's place was a nice, modern apartment building, very much like the one Kris's. Hillhurst was a community trying to revitalize itself into a classy, upscale neighborhood. Thus far they were doing a pretty good job. Kris loved that they had kept most of the maples lining the streets. The sun was out in all its glory today. Kris felt some heat. He also felt cold when it was bad. The light was still a blessing to him. Zeke told him once that things were different for him. He felt neither heat nor cold. He could feel physical things, like the flow of water, or the blowing of the breeze, but not heat or cold. Kris didn't know why he was different. He just was.

Once inside the building, they stood outside the door to Zeke's apartment, which was on the second floor. Kris could smell the scent of blood from outside in the hall, and when Zeke opened the door, the smell was overwhelming. "My god," he said as they stepped inside and Zeke closed the door behind them.

"In the bedroom," Zeke told him, leading the way. Zeke had been a painter during the Renaissance. It was a phase that he never would get past. In some ways that kind of annoyed Kris because Zeke seemed to like to pain him. Not surprisingly on one of his living room walls was a painting of Kris. He remembered that one. It was actually one of Zeke's later works...much later works. Kris had posed for it in the nineteen twenties. All he could remember about it was that he hated that tux. He actually hated all tuxedos, but he hated this one with a vengeance. It was black, as most were, but somehow, even the fact that it was typical didn't matter. Kris glared at Zeke. "You still have that?"

"Yeah, it's one of my favorites," Zeke said, giving Kris a look.

"We'll have to take it when we go. We can't have anyone guessing that we know each other. At least not just yet."

"Fine, whatever," Zeke rolled his eyes and led Kris toward the bedroom.

When he opened the door to the bedroom, Kris nearly fell over upon seeing the blood all over the wall. It was on almost every surface in the room, and there was a thick pool of it around the victim who lay face down in the middle of the floor. The dead man was dressed in jeans, a red tee-shirt, and a ratty brown jacket. It was supposed to look like leather but wasn't.

"Wow," Kris said in a daze, "you're never getting your security deposit back on this place, are you?"

"Sadly no."

"Do you even know the guy's name?" Kris asked.

"Nope."

"Go have a look in his pockets, see if there's a wallet or anything with his ID. And try not to move things around too much. This is a magical crime scene, and neither of us should be here."

"But isn't this the kind of case you work?" Zeke asked, going over the body and rifling through the pockets.

"Considering that the accused is my former lover, they might view it as a conflict of interest. In fact, I shouldn't even be doing this," he said.

"Then why are you?"

"Damned if I know," Kris said. He looked around the room, taking in everything that he could. Zeke had always treated his bedchamber as an oasis of sexual conquest. The large bed with a canopy and thick curtains told Kris that he hadn't changed much. The mere theatrics were hilarious. Then he remembered that he had once been part of those theatrics, and then it wasn't as funny as it had been a moment ago. There was another smaller portrait of him on the bedroom wall. He rolled his eyes. "Why am I always your muse?"

"Oh, c'mon Kris. You have the perfect face for it."

"I haven't got the perfect face for anything," he glanced at it again, "and it's got blood on it. We'll have to take that one too. The MLD can't know that we know each other."

"I found a wallet," Zeke said, "his name is Andrew Lewis."

"Andrew Lewis? Do you remember him now?"

"I think I do," Zeke said quietly, "though I still don't remember leaving with him."

"I don't think we can learn anything else here," Kris said. He had looked everything over, and there was nothing there that could tell them anything more, at least not for now. After they were gone from there, he would call it in and get an evidence team in. He would let them do CSI stuff while he made sure that Zeke stayed safe. "Gather some things. You won't be coming back here for a while."

"Are you arresting me now?" He asked.

"Zeke, people have been disappearing, bodies have been showing up that are obviously the victims of vampires. Even kids are disappearing. This really doesn't look good for you. I should, but I'm not going to."

"Why not?"

"I'm not satisfied that you're guilty."

"Of course, I'm not guilty," Zeke cried, "I'm not a killer! If anything, I'm the very opposite."

Kris rolled his eyes, "you're a lover? Is that it?"

"Something like that."

"I know a place where you can lay low. Once we're out of here, I'm going to call in the magical CSI, and they're going to gather the evidence. I will work the case and try to find out who framed you for murdering this man. Now gather your shit and wipe your fingerprints off the wallet. I have a fucking crime to solve, and you have to disappear, at least for now."

Kris made ready to leave, but then remembered, "Zeke, don't forget to bring the paintings. You really must get over me. I'm a terrible muse."

CHAPTER 3

K ris had stowed Zeke away in an extra apartment he kept on the opposite side of the city for just this very reason. Kris could afford it. He'd lived for over five hundred years and acquired his share of wealth in that time doing a variety of jobs. It was not a large place. One bedroom with a small kitchen, and barely any living room, but it served the purpose of a safe house for people he needed to protect. This was not the first time he'd covered for other vampires. Sometimes even he felt that vampire law needed to be kept separate. After he secured Zeke there he made a call from a payphone down the street from Zeke's place to the MLD and called in the body. Moments later there was a call to Kris's cell phone. Someone had reported a body that seemed to have been killed by a vampire. "No worries," Kris said, "I'll be right there."

Kris waited down the street for the coroner's van to get there and then walked to the building. Lily Watson, the coroner, was getting ready to go in. She was human, one of the few who worked for the MLD. She was sweet and bubbly with her long golden hair and sky-blue eyes. Kris liked her quite a bit but had never gotten up the courage to even ask her out to dinner. Sad really, because he really wanted to.

She smiled at him when he walked up, "you got here fast."

"I live in the neighborhood. Are we the first ones here?"

"Thus far," Lily said, "The investigative team should be here soon, but since we're both here, we might as well go in."

"Alright, are you armed?"

"No, I'm not."

"Then I'll lead the way," Kris said, puffing his chest out a bit. He wasn't really a tough guy, but he knew that he would be much better suited to take down a supernatural attacker should there be one. Also, he knew that there wasn't. He doubted the killer would come back and he knew where Zeke was.

When they opened the door, the scent of the blood hit Kris like a wall again. It was terrible and painful. It would be even worse when they got to the bedroom. His nose curled and he gagged loudly. Lily was taken aback by the fact that the blood was literally everywhere.

"Wow," she said, "this guy is splattered everywhere."

"It would seem so," Kris was gasping, trying to keep from vomiting. The scent was far stronger than it had been before.

"Are you alright?" Lily asked him, "you don't look so well."

"I'm okay," he said, swallowing hard and giving her a little smile, "It's just all the dead blood."

"Just try not to vomit all over the crime scene," she said as she began to look over the body. "This man was bitten once on the neck by a vampire. We'll take a mold of the fangs, but the primary cause of death is blood loss. He was slashed by a razor, which is unusual. He bled out."

"That is really unusual. Vampire's don't slash people with razors, and they certainly don't just let them bleed out."

"This one did."

"I know, it's a damn waste! But it still doesn't make any sense." Kris said kneeling down by the body himself. He still felt a little sick, but he couldn't vomit. Not now. Not in front of her. It would just be more of a bloody mess. She had looked through his clothes and found the wallet. The one thing that truly caught Kris's attention was when she was examining his hands, and a ring with a large ruby fell out of his right hand. She picked the ring up with a pair of tweezers. "Look at this. It has an odd insignia on it."

Kris reached over and grabbed a pair of gloves out of Lily's bag. She dropped the ring into his gloved hand. It was the symbol of Zeke's family, and both he and his sister Anna wore one. He was sure though that Zeke had an emerald stone. He reached into his back pocket and took out his phone, snapping a picture.

"What's that for?" Lily asked him.

"I think I've seen this design before," he said, "who did you say owned this place?"

People began to flood into the room in their gear. There was another detective there. A dragon named Alexander Garner. The two didn't really see eye to eye on most things. In fact, Kris often felt that Alexander would rather compete than work together on anything.

"You know what, never mind," Kris said, "I think I've seen everything I need to."

"But what about the murder weapon?" She asked.

"You're not going to find it," Kris said, "or at least I don't think you will. This was a professional job, as crimes by vamps go. You and Garner can look for it if you want to."

"But he'll get all the credit."

"Don't worry about it," Kris told her, "I have to go see a man about a ring."

"What do you mean? Do you know whose ring that is?"

"I suspect," he said, getting to his feet, "and that is a start. Carry on!" He said as he made his way across the room. Garner glanced at him with dark, suspicious eyes, but did not speak to him. Kris was glad. He really didn't want to talk to that asshole.

***

Garner wondered where Kris was off to so quickly after his arrival. He thought the vampire was an annoying know-it-all. He walked over to where Lily was still examining the body.

"Where's Kellman off to in such a hurry?"

"He got here early. Said he needed to see a man about a ring."

"What ring?"

Lily held up the ring in her gloves hand. "This ring. He's probably off to see a jeweler."

"I don't know about that," Garner said, "it might be that he knows who owns it and has gone to warn them or something."

"Are you being all suspicious again?" He could tell by the look on her face that she was not amused by his deductions.

"Well, how did he get here so fast?"

"I think he lives around here."

"I think a lot of them do. The vamps. It makes sense that they would take care of their own. People have been disappearing, and there has been a lot of vamp movement recently."

"Oh, don't be that way," Lily said, as she got to her feet, "I'm done here. But you've gotta stop with this thing you have against vampires. They're not bad creatures. Nor are dragons."

"You should see me in my true form. Golden scales and all," he said. He was proud of his true dragon form, though he didn't get to share it often.

"I'm sure I would be quite pleased, but for now, I've got to take care of this body, and the MLD people have to cast their magic and make this place look like someone didn't blow up an animal in here."

"Yeah," he said, "we'll talk later." He kind of liked this woman. She seemed like a sweet, classy lady. He liked that. One of the other things that he and Kellman were at odds about. God that vampire was a dick.

Then he noticed something odd. There were many portraits in the apartment that looked to have been painted by the same artists. There was a void in some of the blood-spattered on the wall. Someone had removed one of the paintings from the bedroom. He went out to the living room, and there seemed to be another place where a painting was missing from its spot. Had this been some kind of robbery gone wrong? Had thieves come here to steal art and ended up accidentally killing this man instead? Had the man been the thief? All questions that needed answering. And Garner hated unanswered questions.

***

Kris opened the door to the spare apartment. As he stepped in through the door, he remembered what a hole in the wall it was. Tiny, dingy and dark. It wasn't really a living space. It was a space to keep people who needed to hide. Kris hated it, as did Zeke who was sitting on the puffy brown sofa staring at a crack in the wall. "If you're trying to make the crack bigger with your mind, I don't think it works that way," Kris said.

Zeke glanced up at him and then looked back at the crack. "So, what have you found out?" He asked.

Kris pulled out his phone and brought up the picture of the ring, "you recognize this?"

"Yeah, I do," Zeke reached up and grabbed the phone, staring at it in disbelief. "How can this be?"

"You're still wearing yours, right?"

Zeke lifted his hand and showed Kris the ring. It had a large emerald stone in it, as Kris remembered. Kris sat in the ugly grey chair opposite Zeke. "It's Anna's, isn't it?"

"Yes..."

"Your sister set you up."

"Yeah, she did. She's been planning to for some time."

"Wait," Kris said, confused. "She's been planning to do this to you?"

"Well, yeah."

"And you didn't think to tell me this before?" Kris was baffled.

"She's family, Kris. I take care of her when I can. I didn't want to say."

"You didn't want to say?!" Kris put his head in his hands, "Goddammit, you're daft sometimes."

"I didn't want it to be her, Kris!" Zeke was now angry as well. He slapped his hand down on one of the cushy sofa arms, making a loud slapping sound. Kris hadn't seen him this angry since the night they had broken up. "I didn't want to think that my sister was a murderer, or that she set me up for that murder. I'm sorry. I shouldn't have snapped."

"Nor should I have," Kris said, "I suppose I can understand since she is your sister. What is going on here? Why would she set you up?"

"Things have changed, Kris. Charles Anderson wants vampires to be on the top of the food chain. He's working toward that. I'm standing in his way, as would you if you still had anything to do with the community. She didn't want to kill me herself, but she knows that if I'm in prison, I won't be able to stop Charles. She loves him, Kris."

"She loves him?"

"Yes, and you know how deeply she can love."

"Yes, I do. I'm surprised to hear that Charles is at it again. Remember when you found me back in the fourteen hundreds?" Kris gave a long sigh, "I was his blood slave and one of his victims in attempting to make vampires dominant. He didn't mean to turn me. He had to because a friend of his bit me. He wasn't supposed to. I have no idea why Charles chose to turn me instead of letting me die."

"Yeah, I forgot about that," Zeke mused. "You know you could still press charges against him for turning you without consent. The MLD has laws about that now. Vampires always have, but now it's law recognized by the magic police."

Kris groaned. He didn't want to have this conversation again. Zeke had tried, on multiple occasions, to get Kris to report Charles. "I would love to stay and chat, but now I have to go. I think I know where I can find her and I need to go find something to wear."

"You going clubbing?"

"Yeah. You know the place."

"I think I do. Damn, I wish I could go with you," a depressed look crossed Zeke's face.

"But sadly, you can't. You have to be a good boy and stay here. Do as you're told. Try and make that crack bigger with your mind."

"I hate you sometimes," Zeke said.

"Yeah, I know." And then he was gone.

CHAPTER 4

The night was clear and brisk. Kris could clearly see his breath when he got out of his black BMW outside of the Midnight Bliss Club. Standing at the door was someone he knew far better than he cared to remember. "Damn, not him," Kris said. This was the second ex he had run into today. Ross was a dragon. A mega-monster who was actually capable of breathing fire. He was also capable of wounding by way of infidelity, but Kris didn't want to remember that. He just wanted to go in and ask a few people a few questions. "Hello, Ross," he said, approaching the dragon.

"Kris?" Ross asked. There was a baffled look behind his dark-rimmed glasses. "I haven't seen you in a while."

"Yeah, it's been about twenty years. Is there any chance that we could have a chat?"

"Sure," Ross said, "I think I know what this is about. We probably shouldn't be doing this here, but there's really no place else. Go on in, I'll come find you in a moment."

"Right," Kris said. He entered the club. It was loud, with annoying repetitious music that would have given Kris a headache if he could still get those. It was dark and ugly. All of the walls had been done in a gross purple color, and all of the tables, floors and even the bar were all in weird off shades of violet. *Charles never did have any taste.*

He went and sat at a little table as far from the dance floor as he could. He wasn't interested in service, he'd come to speak with Ross and he planned to do so. There were all kinds of different creatures in there. Dragons blowing smoke rings, vampires feeding on willing participants, witches and warlocks trading spells, and a few people like Kris who really didn't want to be noticed. He was a boring suit and tie guy anyway. People wouldn't notice him. And with the thick smoke and loud music, people could barely see each other as it was. A moment later, he was joined by Ross.

"Sorry about that. Had to get someone else to watch the door."

"No problem," Kris said.

"You wanted to talk to me about something?"

"A murder that occurred today in my neighborhood."

"I heard about it," Ross said.

"They think it was Zeke."

"It wasn't Zeke," Ross said, "Zeke's a dipshit, not a murderer."

"Agreed on that," Kris said, having a look around for anyone suspicious. "I don't want it to be Anna, but I think it might be."

"Anna? His sister Anna?"

"Yes. I'm pretty sure that she's not alone in this."

"Charles, right?"

"Charles was always a dick. I am going to guess that he hasn't changed."

"You wouldn't be wrong," Ross said blowing a ring of smoke out of his nose. "He's gone mad these days. Has a "plan for all vampires" that makes them kings on this Earth. He's also trying to rid himself of anyone who stands in his way."

"That's what he was doing the first time we met," Kris shuddered to remember it, "it didn't work then, and it won't work now. He has no right to kill humans. He had no right to kill me and bring me back."

"And yet that is what he's planning to do. Damn humans. They just get in the way, don't they?"

"Yes, but that doesn't mean that if they find out about this, they won't go on a crusade to destroy us. They may appear useless, but they're far more destructive than any "monster" they may fear. The MLD will be glad to know about Charles's."

"As of yet, you can't prove anything," Ross said, "If you confront Charles, he can easily deny given that anyone who has stood in his way has been dealt with. There are rumors that he's kidnapped several of his fellow vamps and has done something with them that's both terrible and illegal. Even Zeke is in a bad place right now. Given the evidence against him and nothing connecting him to Charles or Anna, you don't have a leg to stand on."

"There might be," Kris said, taking out his phone. He pulled up the picture of Anna's ring. "Technically we can connect Anna to the scene. This is her ring. I have other pictures, ancient ones in a safe place that clearly show her wearing the ring."

Ross gave Kris a hard look, "why are you telling me all this?"

"At first, I didn't want to. The moment I saw you standing out there, I was reminded of things I didn't want to remember. Which is why I'm going to ask you this question. Are you his? Are you Charles's? Does he hold any sway over you at all?"

"No, I'm not, and no he doesn't. Get on with it!"

Kris leaned across the table, "I need an ally in this escapade. If anything should happen to me, I need someone who knows the connection between Anna and the ring. Hopefully, the pictures will clear Zeke, but only if someone else knows where they are. If I can't stop this, then I need to know that he can be saved. If the vamps know I'm trying to save Zeke, they'll target me next."

"Are you thinking of confronting Anna and Charles? That's insane! They won't listen to you, and they have far too many people on their side now."

"I know, but if I can stop this before it gets too far out of hand..."

"My God, Kris. And you're doing this for Zeke?"

Kris sighed, "I still care for him, just as I still care for you."

"And what about Anna?"

"She was always a manipulative bitch," Kris said, "I won't miss her if she should go down for this murder."

"What's the plan?" Ross asked, he looked as though he really didn't want any part of this, but Kris had no choice.

Kris handed him an envelope, "Inside this envelope is an account number and a key to a safety deposit box at the RBC Royal Bank on Sage Hill Plaza. You know the one, right?"

"Yeah, I think so," Ross said, "the pictures are in there?"

"Yes."

"You're keeping pictures in a safety deposit box?"

"Yes, in case of something just like this."

Ross gave a loud laugh and kept laughing, "You cheeky little wanker. You're devious like the rest of us, aren't you?" He and Kris were still Londoners at heart. Sometimes, Kris even missed it after forty years away.

"Oh, I don't know about that," Kris said, "let's say that I won't lose any sleep if Anna goes to prison. She killed someone; it's not the first time. This time around she needs to face the consequences."

"Admit it! You'd love it!"

"You're right," Kris laughed, "in some ways, I'm no better than anyone else. But this is not about us. This is about her disregard for the law."

"Well, maybe you can ask her about it," Ross said, pointing behind Kris, "she's headed this way."

Kris looked over his shoulder, and there she was in a long red dress wearing bright red heels. She looked gorgeous with her beautiful black hair cascading over her shoulders. God, he hated her. She walked up behind him and put her hand on his shoulder. "Hello, Kris," she said digging her nails in.

"Get your claws off me, please," he reached up and knocked her hand away," I'm in no mood to be mauled by a feral cat."

"Then why are you here?" She asked, she grabbed a chair from a nearby table and sat down at Kris's table.

Kris looked at her hand, the one he knew she wore the ring on. "Not wearing your ring?" He asked.

"No," she said with a sly smile, "I seem to have lost it somewhere."

"I think I may have found it for you," Kris said, "at Zeke's place."

"Really?" She said, "I haven't seen Zeke in a while."

"Both you and I know that's a lie."

"Do we?" She asked, putting her hand on his shoulder again, she leaned in and whispered into his ear, "you know nothing. Trust me, it's best that way."

"I know more than you think," he swatted her hand away again, "and whatever you and Charles are doing, I suggest you stop now. We have your ring, and I have proof that it's yours. I would really like to discuss what's happening with Charles."

"Charles is out of town. I suggest you not get in his way."

"That's not the way the law works, dear."

"It is if you wish to keep living."

"Both you and Charles should know it's not wise to make threats against law enforcement."

"Be careful, Kris," Anna said as she rose from her chair, "bad things can sometimes happen to nosy people."

"Do they?" He asked, "that's sad."

"You have no idea," she said as she rose and began to walk away.

"Well, I need to get back," Ross said as he got up as well. He hesitated for a moment, "she's right. You should be careful, Kris."

"Don't worry," Kris said, "I'll be careful."

CHAPTER 5

It was eight o'clock or so when Kris returned to the MLD. He didn't really want to, but he wanted to know what was happening with the investigation. The building was enchanted. From the outside, it looked like a broken-down apartment building. There were jagged, broken windows and graffiti on the red brick walls. Kris went to the front door. When he opened it and stepped inside, he stepped onto clean, black tile floors. The walls were bright white. For a vampire, they were almost blinding especially with the lights as bright as they were. He tried not to look at them.

He walked down another hall that led to the stairs leading to the morgue. He liked the basement far better. The only lights he had to deal with there were the lights Lily used to illuminate the body. He made his way down the stairs and into the hallway. He pushed his way through the double doors and found Lily still examining the body. Unfortunately, Garner was right there by her side. "Where have you been?" Garner looked annoyed. He didn't like it when Kris went off and did his own thing. Kris couldn't help it. That was just the way he was.

"What's it matter to you?" He asked, annoyed by Garner's annoyance. "Following up on a lead. It was a dead end."

"A lead you didn't tell anyone about turned out to be bogus? Sounds like your kind of investigation technique. How long has it been since you've solved a case?"

"Stop," Lily said, "I don't want to hear it. The body is also a dead end. Nothing else to report. No evidence on it, the cause of death is apparent. It just doesn't make sense. Someone wanted to murder this guy. If it was a vampire, why wouldn't they kill him like a vampire?"

"The logic doesn't make sense to me either," It was true. A vampire not killing like a vampire was an anomaly. "That might be a good thing, though. If we can find similar murders that don't involve vampires killing like vampires, it may lead us to something."

"That's a good idea," Garner smirked at him. Kris didn't like the look in his eye, "why don't you look into that? You're a vamp, right? Sounds right up your alley to try and bring down other vamps."

That would take a ridiculous amount of time, "I'll get on it tomorrow."

"Good, it ought to keep you from disappearing again."

"I didn't disappear. I told you what I was doing."

"Yeah, whatever. I'm going to try and find this guy, Ezekiel Yonah."

"He won't go back to his place," Kris said, "It's been enchanted, but he would still smell the dead blood. It almost made me vomit. He won't be coming back."

"Do you know this guy?" Garner asked.

That really pissed Kris off. "Oh yeah, dipshit, all vampires know each other. That's vampire racist."

"I was just asking because you live in the same neighborhood."

That was a reasonable assumption. Or at least it was somewhat understandable. "No," Kris said, knowing he had overreacted, "I don't know him."

"You two need to go home," Lily said, "I can't stand listening to you two arguing like children."

"Sorry," Kris said, "I've done wrong..." He shook his head, "yeah, I'm going home."

"Get some sleep."

"Not likely," he told her, "I've got things on my mind."

She smiled at him, "don't we all?"

He gave a laugh, "best of nights to you."

It was best not to say anything to Garner. It wasn't worth it to Kris. He was also hungry. That was exasperating too. And tomorrow he also had to do research into suspects. He already knew who was responsible. Everything was a pain tonight.

His car was parked a couple of blocks down. No one parked in front of the building to keep people from wondering why. It was a beautiful night to take a walk. The stars were beautiful in the clear spring sky. Kris was looking up and didn't see the person who bumped into him. He did notice the note that was pressed into his hand by whoever passed by.

The note was obvious: *Leave this alone or face the consequences. You have been warned.*

A threat. They were not at all afraid to issue it. The vampire leadership was onto him. He had to be careful now. If Charles's people tried to take him, there would be no one to watch over Zeke. He would never give up, but now things were complicated. Charles wouldn't hesitate to hurt him.

He walked to his car. Head down and eyes forward from now on. They would be watching him.

***

Thankfully, he found Zeke right where he had left him at the apartment. Kris could only stay here tonight, and then he would have to go back to his place. Staying at another place might raise suspicions. He was pretty sure that Garner didn't trust him and would love to find him in violation of the law. Harboring a suspect would be a violation. Zeke was already asleep on the sofa when he came in. Kris paid him no mind at first and went to the refrigerator. There were bags of blood in the fridge. Thankfully, vampires knew guys who could get it for them.

Kris didn't like drinking straight from the bag so poured it into a wine glass. Much better. He took the glass and sat down in the worn-looking chair across from Zeke. He liked to watch Zeke sleep. He looked like an angel curled up on that sofa. Kris sat there, sipping the blood and watching. He remembered a time when he and Zeke had been happy together. Now that was a distant memory. Then again, here he was, helping Zeke to avoid a murder conviction. Kris sighed.

He fell asleep in that chair. When he woke up, he found Zeke sitting and watching him sleep.

"You alright?" Zeke asked.

"I don't know," Kris said, "I received a threat last night from Charles and his people. Garner hates me. It's okay, I hate him too. Puff the Magic Dragon needs to fuck off."

"I don't know who that is."

"Lucky you..."

"I want to thank you again for helping me," Zeke said, "I don't deserve it."

"Yeah, I know."

Zeke smiled, "I should just turn myself in."

"I worry that they might try to get to you while incarcerated."

"How do you think they'd do that?"

"I don't know, but I don't feel like taking the risk. Charles has reach. I don't want to think that he's infiltrated The Vampire Council in Montreal, but it's entirely possible that he has. Leadership here should have shut him and his crap down years ago."

"Look at you being all paranoid," Zeke gave a laugh.

Kris was incensed, "I'm not paranoid. I'm careful."

"Yes, I am well aware of how careful you are," Zeke said.

Kris shook his head, "I need to get ready for work. I have to research possible suspects."

"That sounds boring."

"This is all your fault," Kris got up, "Now I have to go back to my place and find clothes. It's five in the morning. I don't usually get up this early."

"Kris, trust me you have clothes. You probably have everything labeled. It's not that much of a hardship. Like someone as OCD as you forgets to do the laundry."

"Yeah, I was really OCD when I was putting together files on everyone. Locked away in a safe place. You should see your file. I have some really amusing pictures of you."

"Not those," Zeke said worriedly.

"I have photo evidence of what a fun drunk you are. Aren't you glad we can still get drunk?"

"You still have those? I will fucking kill you. Where are they?"

"Can't tell you."

"You're a real bastard sometimes; you know that?"

"Yeah, I know. Pain in the ass, eh?" Sometimes Kris worried that he was becoming too Canadian. "Anyway, clothes, work, research and then I have to go to my place."

"Right," Zeke said. "I can hold out here."

"Whatever. Just don't leave the apartment."

"I'm not a fool."

"That's debatable."

"You jerk!"

"Yeah, I love you too, snuggle bunny. Later!" Kris left. Fighting with Zeke was adorable, but he really had to get on with things.

CHAPTER 6

Kris didn't want to go into work that morning. He knew that Garner would want exactly what he had asked for, which would mean the endless reading of files all day looking for connections that he knew wouldn't be there. He found them at his desk when he got there. "Damn," he said out loud to himself.

"That looks like a pain," Kris almost jumped out of his skin when he heard the voice behind him. He swung around and found Lily standing there.

"Good lord, you scared me," Kris said, holding his chest.

"Sure, but I doubt you're at any risk of having a heart attack."

Kris laughed, "yeah, I figure you're right."

"That's quite a pile of work you've got to go through."

"Yeah, I don't know if I'm going to find anything in this pile of bull shit. Still, I guess it's worth a look."

"It's unusual," Lily said, "if there were other cases like this, they would certainly stand out."

"Oh, I'm sure," Kris said. He sat down at his desk. His old chair squeaked as he sat down, "I really need to get this thing replaced. I'm going to assume that Garner's already been here."

"He has," Lily said, "he really wants to find this Yonah guy."

"Yonah is probably long gone by now," Kris said, "I would be if I had done something like this and there was no way out."

"You figure he's guilty?"

"I wouldn't know. It looks like it."

"Some part of me really wants to believe he's innocent," Lily said.

Kris looked up at her in surprise. "Really?"

"Yeah, really."

"Some part of me hopes you're right," Kris said, "as a fellow vampire, I would just like him to be innocent, but I don't see how it would work out that way."

"Well, when, or if we find him, we can ask him."

"Sure, I guess," Kris looked over at his stack of files, "until then."

"Have fun," Lily said, and then she left him to his work.

He was through about half of them by the time lunch came around. In that time, he had found maybe three or four that seemed similar out of a hundred. His vampire's eyes read far more swiftly than human eyes. They were all unsolved; humans that appeared to be killed by vamps, but with no apparent perpetrator. They had shown up in alleys and on dark night streets and in dark corners of parks and forests in the night. Zeke's was the first one where the murder could possibly be tied to an actual person. They had all happened within the last five years, and now they could all potentially be tied to Zeke. He knew who was behind them. They had been setting this up for some time. He couldn't go to the bosses with this. At least not yet. He knew that what he was doing was not right and that he was hindering an investigation. He felt that he had to for Zeke.

He put those files in his desk drawer before he got up to leave for lunch. Guilt ate at him. This is the first time he had ever been dishonest during an investigation, and he could certainly lose his job over this. He got up and made his way out. The white walls almost blinded him again. *Fucking white walls...*

He was walking down the street toward his car when he felt someone come up behind him again. Instead of just leaving a note, his arm was grabbed, and he was pulled rapidly down the street and was pushed into the back seat of a strange car that had been waiting. He knew the driver well. It was Anna. As for his vampire-napper, it was a small woman with dark hair who now had a gun pointed at his chest.

"There must be some kind of misunderstanding," he said, "I know Anna, but I don't know who you are, or what you want. But you're not going to kill me by shooting me."

"Who says I want to kill you?" She asked in a high pitched nasally voice, "maybe I just want to teach you a lesson."

"What lesson would that be?" Kris rolled his eyes.

"You've been a bad boy," Anna said over her shoulder, "you deserve to be punished."

"What is this all about?" Kris asked.

"Charles is back, and he wishes to speak with you," Anna said.

"He has my number. He could have just called."

"Well, you know how much he likes theatrics."

"I remember. Zeke says you love him."

"Zeke is a fool."

"He's your brother, you heartless bitch!" Kris was no longer amused.

"And that somehow makes him less of a fool?"

He couldn't help but feel she was right in some way, "he's a good guy."

"I didn't say he wasn't."

"I hate it when you talk in little circles."

"What does it matter? It's not like we have anything to really discuss."

"Oh sure, we have nothing to discuss. You just vampire-napped me, you crazy person."

"Bitch, bitch, bitch..."

They pulled up in front of a high-end looking apartment building. Kris could afford a place like this, but it was far too expensive looking for a frugal, simple guy like him. What he needed was far more useful than what others wanted. An uncomfortable elevator ride to the twelfth floor finally brought him to the top. A short way down a white hall, they came to a door. Anna opened it, and Kris was pushed through by the woman with the gun. Charles was sitting on a large black sofa against a large bay of windows.

He was roughly escorted to an armchair across from Charles who was sitting there like a king, a sinister smile on his face. Kris glared at the gun-wielding woman who stood by his side, still pointing the gun at him. Anna went and sat next to Charles who put his arm around her.

Kris pointed at the gun-wielding woman, "where did you pick this one up? She's the bossiest vamp I've had to deal with since Anna. She does know that the gun won't really hurt me, right?"

"Oh, I don't know about that," Charles said, "it still hurts, it just won't kill you. Most of the time."

"Most of the time? What the hell does that mean?"

"It doesn't matter now. We have other things to discuss."

"Oh, you want to have a discussion," Kris said, "you're not just being a giant dick for the purpose of being a giant dick? What do you want, Charles?"

"We need you to give up Zeke."

"Why?"

"He's in the way and he needs to be removed."

"Why?"

"Will you please stop it. You're being annoying."

"I'm being annoying?" Kris said, "Me? Did I vampire-nap you in the middle of the day just to bother you with bullshit?"

"You will do as I ask, Kris," Charles was getting that dangerous look in his eye again. Kris had seen it several times in his long life, and it never led to anything good. "I heard you were keeping information on us all. We tried to get it from our mutual friend Ross, but he's not someone we can easily deal with. He has friends who could end us, so it's best to try and get it from you."

"I do. I'm not giving you anything."

"Kris, if you get in our way, we will deal with you, and it will not be pretty."

"Are you threatening me?"

"Does it sound like I am?"

"Sorta, and threatening law enforcement isn't wise."

"Oh sure," Charles said, "but you and I both know that if we decide to deal with you, the chances that they could help you is slim. You would disappear, and no one would ever find you."

"Does the Vampire Council in Montreal know what you're up to? That you're making members of your own people "disappear?""

"The Council is weak. I was just with them, and they said they weren't going to get in my way. In fact, half of them were with me."

"Dipshits who don't know how dangerous this is for all creatures. If humans feel that they're in danger, they will destroy us." Kris glared at the vampire, "how could you betray your own kind?"

"You were always so dramatic, Kris," Charles rolled his eyes, "like the way you screamed the night that I killed your wife and took you."

"You asshole piece of shit."

"Listen to reason, Kris! You can't stop me, so you might as well join me."

"I'm not telling you anything, but I will make you an offer. Stop what you're doing, I'll help to make Zeke disappear. That way we can all keep on living, and hopefully, this will eventually go away."

"Kris, you're in no position to be making deals or threats."

"Oh yeah?"

"Oh yeah," Charles glared at him. "Now get out."

Kris was escorted out as unpleasantly as he was escorted in. When they dropped him off back at the MLD, the vampire woman basically kicked him out of the car. He didn't fall to the ground as they had intended. He flipped off the car as it drove away. He would go hungry for now. He had to get back. *Fucking Charles...*

***

Kris had made his way through most of the files by the end of the day. He hadn't found any more cases that were like Zeke's, which was a good thing. Garner had returned and made his way over to Kris's desk. "You find anything?"

Kris jumped, not seeing the dragon at first. When he had calmed himself, he said, "anything relevant? Not to this case. Nothing similar. Good lord, you're quiet. The idea of stealth dragons freaks me out."

"Good. That's good. No luck in tracking down Yonah, but I went back to his place. We found a witness that said that he did return to the apartment after the murder."

"Did he?" Kris froze. If someone had seen them...

"That's what she said," Garner gave him a hard look, "she said he was with someone. The person she described sounds a bit like you."

"Really," had he been busted? "And what is this witness's name?"

"I don't remember. Some lady with black hair, kind of short. I think her name was Sandra or something."

"I see," Charles was just getting started, "well it wasn't me. I said I don't know the guy and I don't."

"Alright, whatever," the dragon huffed a smoke ring out of his nose. Kris knew Garner didn't believe him.

"So basically, we still have nothing?" Kris was glad. He knew what had happened already. He also didn't want lizard lips to have any wins. It was a little immature and petty, but he hated the dragon.

"Looks that way." The dragon's claws sprang from the ends of his fingers, and he began to drum them on Kris's desk.

"I hate having nothing." Kris gave him a little grin. He hoped it looked a little sincere.

"You and me both," Garner retracted his claws, "well, I'll be seeing you. I'm taking Lily out tonight."

"Are you?" Kris's face burned with jealousy. He hated that he was jealous of that idiot, but he was. He forced himself to smile. It was never wise to make an enemy of a dragon.

"Yup, see you tomorrow."

"Oh sure, see you." Garner wandered away, and Kris's smile dropped immediately.

Fucking Garner...

***

Sandra was an assassin. She had been one since well before she had become a vampire and had continued to do it in the service of Charles. She was sitting in her car, watching the street outside of Kris Kellman's apartment. She didn't like him. She would love it when Charles gave the order. When she got the call, she expected just that. She answered the phone, "hello."

"Sandra," Charles's voice came over the phone, "I need something from you."

"Kellman's death?"

"Not yet," he said, "the pieces are moving. I don't want you to kill him yet. I need you to teach him a lesson. A lesson only. You have the special bullets I gave you, right?"

"I do," she said.

"Give me two days, then teach him a lesson he won't soon forget."

"I want to kill him now," she said.

"I know you do, but it's not time just yet. Can you do this for me?"

"Anything you need, my love."

"Splendid," he said. He ended the call. She would have to wait and she hated waiting.

***

Kris spent the rest of the week going through more files and interviewing people who had nothing interesting to tell him. Also, he had to watch as Garner and Lily together, which was kind of annoying. *Well, you should have asked her out when you had the chance, idiot.*

One morning, Garner came over to Kris's desk, a vase of flowers in hand. Kris didn't know what this was about, and he wasn't really amused by it. "Wow, I never knew you were interested. Sadly, you're not my type."

"These are not for you. Do you think Lily will like them?"

Kris lifted an eyebrow. Did Garner want his opinion? He looked at the assortment of yellow roses and orange lilies. "That's certainly impressive. I think she'll like the lilies. Other than that, how the fuck should I know? If you're not into me, why should I care?"

"You're right, never mind."

"You know I'm not the only guy who works here. Go ask Brianna. She's a fairy; she loves shiny objects and stuff like that."

"Shiny objects?" Garner huffed smoke out of his nose again. He seemed to like that move. "And you're the one claiming I'm racist against vampires."

"You are racist against vampires."

"Am not."

"Go bother someone else," Kris didn't have time for this. Well actually he did, but he didn't want to. "Go give her your flowers. I'm sure she'll love them...or something..."

"Yeah," Garner said, "whatever." He walked away.

Kris flipped him off under the desk, "douche bag."

He didn't hear Captain Alison Harris coming up behind him. He jumped when he felt her hand on his shoulder. He spun around in his chair to face a tall, blond woman with golden translucent wings. "Good lord, feren are sneaky. You scared me to death."

"Not likely," she laughed, her voice was beautiful and melodic, "so how are things going with the investigation?"

"Well enough, I guess. I've been going through endless files and not finding any similar cases, questioning people who have nothing to tell me. Meanwhile, Garner is pounding the pavement and accomplishing absolutely nothing."

"That's disappointing," She said, shaking her head, "I just wish we could find this Yonah guy so that we can hear from him what happened."

"He's probably long gone by now. As a vampire, he's probably pretty good at disappearing." Kris felt terrible that he had to lie to Harris. He liked her. She was good at what she did, and they had been working together for forty years. Almost since the day he'd arrived in Calgary. She trusted him, and that would all go out the window if she found out he was lying to her.

"You're right about that, I know well enough how annoying it can be to catch a magical predator." Kris nodded. They had taken out some pretty crazy creatures together over the years. His memory drifted to a time when they had teamed up to take out a den of murderous werewolves who had been preying on the city at night. Ah, those were the days.

"Yeah, I know. We'll keep at it."

"Do that," she said. She put her hand on his shoulder, "and Kris, saying that fairies are attracted to shiny objects is a stereotype that people such as myself don't appreciate."

Kris laughed, "damn your fairy ears. Sorry about that. I just wanted to get rid of him."

"He hates you so much," she chuckled.

"Yeah, I know."

"I do wish you would get along, but chances are that's not going to happen."

"Not a chance, sadly."

"Well, keep at it, and hopefully we'll get this done, right?"

"Right," Kris said, "thank you, Captain."

"Carry on," she left him to his work.

It was the end of the week, and he felt it was a good idea to go see how Zeke was doing. When he opened the door to the spare apartment, he didn't see Zeke at first. *That idiot hasn't left the house, has he?* Kris walked quickly to the back of the apartment and looked into the small bedroom. There he found Zeke, lying on the bed staring at the ceiling. He looked over when he heard Kris come in. "Oh, it's you," he said, not even looking over at Kris, "I am so bored. Where have you been?"

"Working."

"Working? You've been working and have left me here to languish in solitude."

"You're such a drama queen," Kris said as he came over and sat on the bed, "you hungry?"

"Oh, I guess."

"I'll go and see if we have anything in the refrigerator."

"I'm lucky you came around," Zeke said, looking over at Kris, "I think we're out."

"What do you mean we're out?" Kris asked, annoyed. "There was a month's worth in the fridge."

"I was bored."

"So, you gorged?"

"I've been painting with it," Zeke said. He pointed into the bathroom. Kris got up from the bed and walked into the bathroom. There, on the wall was an intricate painting of a dragon fighting a lion and the words, "epic dragon fight," in blood. There was also a small portrait of Kris's face above the dragon and the lion; like he was the sun shining over the two fighting creatures. It was God awful, or at least Kris thought so. Kris's mouth fell open. "Oh my God."

"Do you like it?" Zeke asked. During the Renaissance, he had studied painting but had never become an artist of import for obvious reasons. He still had the skills, though. The beautiful portrait of Kris's face smiled back at him.

Kris stalked out of the bathroom. He glared down at Zeke, "you ruined my wall. And why on earth am I your muse, you ridiculous cretin? You know I hate pictures of myself. I'm going to my place, and I'll bring some more back."

"Whatever." Zeke rolled over and ignored Kris, "and you've always been my muse. You know why!"

"You know I'm doing all of this for you, right?"

Zeke rolled over again and smiled at Kris. "I know, thanks for your help."

Kris rolled his eyes, "whatever..." He left the apartment and went back to his apartment where he got his emergency stash of blood out of the fridge. *Fucking Zeke.*

He drove back over to the other apartment. Thankfully he didn't have to work tomorrow. He could use a good rest. He got out and started to rummage in the back seat where he had set the box with the blood bags. He was grabbed from behind and was thrown to the ground. He rolled onto his back and saw the vampire woman, Sandra standing over him. She was pointing the gun at him again. He scrambled to his feet. "You again," he said, "has Charles sent you to kill me? You can't kill me with your gun, remember?"

"We'll see about that," she said. She pulled the trigger. He was already moving before the gun had fired. He hoped that with his vampire speed he could escape the bullets. He was sure they had missed him when he ran and tried to disappear into the darkness. She gave chase, firing off a few more, but he was gone down a dark alley. He made his way to the roof of the building by way of a quick jog up the wall. Thankfully it was already dark, and he had to hope that no humans had witnessed what had happened. Sometimes being magical was a pain in the ass. Once on the roof, he went to the fire ladder and made his way down. He broke his own window to get into the apartment. He fell onto the living room floor in front of Zeke who had an astonished look on his face.

"Kris?" He said, "what the hell?" He ran to Kris's side.

"I just ran away from a crazy lady with a gun. She hasn't followed me, and she seems to have missed."

Zeke pointed at a dark stain on Kris's light blue shirt, "no she didn't. You've been shot. Don't worry, though, it'll heal."

"Will it?" Kris asked as he looked down at the wound. "I'm bleeding pretty badly," he said, "I need blood."

"Unless you brought some with you, we don't have any."

"Down in my car. It's down in my car," Kris said. Moments later, he collapsed. Zeke rushed to his side and picked him up. Kris was barely conscious as he felt Zeke lay him down on the bed in the bedroom. He reached his hand into his pocket and took out his car keys, "go down to the car and get the supply."

"You think it's safe out there?"

"Are you really wussing out right now?"

"What? No..."

"Then go," Kris knew it was a risk, but he knew Zeke had to do this.

"Right," Zeke said. Zeke sped out of the room at top speed. Being a vampire had its perks. Kris laid there. His wound wasn't healing and the seeping blood was ruining the mattress. Moments later, Zeke was back. He had one of the blood bags in his hand. He bit off the end of the hose to open it. He then stuck it in Kris's mouth. The wound wasn't healing. It wasn't bleeding as badly, but it was still bleeding. Zeke ripped open Kris's shirt. Kris grunted as he heard it rip. He watched as Zeke leaned over him and sniffed the wound. "I'm going to drink off you," he said.

"What?" Kris asked.

"Dead man's blood," Zeke said. He bit into Kris's wrist.

Kris cried out. It had been a while. "Goddammit!"

Zeke's lips came away from Kris's wrist. "Goddammit is right and so was I. The bullet must have been laced with dead man's blood."

"How is that possible?" Kris asked blearily.

"I don't know, but we've got to get it out of you, or you'll bleed to death."

"What?" Kris asked. He wasn't tracking things very well at the moment. "Are you a doctor?"

"No Kris, I'm a vampire. Dead man's blood is poison. It's making the wound so that it won't heal. It's making the would mortal. That means that you can and will bleed to death if it isn't treated as a mortal wound."

Kris passed out and didn't hear the rest of what Zeke was trying to say.

***

Zeke was panicking. Kris had passed out, and he had no idea what he was going to do. "Kris, you asshole! Wake up!" He shook Kris, but the other vampire didn't react. "Goddammit, I am so screwed..." He had to think of something. He searched through Kris's pockets and pulled out his phone. Kris had to know someone, anyone, who could help. He looked through the contacts. The one right at the top of the list was "Lily." Zeke was sure that he remembered Kris having spoken about her and that she was a doctor...or something. "Damn," he said as he pressed call. It was a risk, but one he had to make.

"Hello Kris," he heard a woman's voice say as someone answered.

"You're Lily?" He asked.

"Yes, who's this? I know Kris's voice, and you're not Kris."

"Kris has been hurt, and it's not healing. He needs help, or he's going to bleed out, and I can't help him."

"I will help him, but first, who are you?"

"I can't tell you that, but know that he trusts me, and you can as well. I will text you the address. Please come." He ended the call and sent the text. He knew that she might not come. Kris would die if she didn't, but she had no reason to trust him. Kris's wound continued to bleed. Tears ran from Zeke's eyes. It terrified him that this might kill Kris.

Twenty minutes later there was a knock on the door. He went and looked nervously out the peephole. There was a small blond woman standing out in the hall with a concerned look on her face. "Lily?" He asked.

"You called for me? I'm here to help Kris," she said through the door.

He opened the door. Hopefully, it was not too late.

***

Kris opened his eyes and he was still alive. Being shot wasn't something that he was new to. Being close to death was something he hadn't experienced in five hundred years. He tried to move but found that it was best that he didn't. He hadn't felt this wounded in a long time. It was as if he was experiencing the same thing a human did when they were hit by bullets. He reached his hand down to feel it and felt bandages. The wound was definitely still there. It was treated as if it were a human wound. *What the hell happened to me?*

He heard voices in the other room. One was Zeke's, and the other was Lily's. What was Lily doing here? He tried to listen as best he could.

"He's going to live," Lily said, "or at least I think he should. Just keep him fed, and he should recover."

"Thank you for coming. I know it must have been difficult to get a call from a stranger and come to them not knowing what you'll find. I thank you for that."

"It was actually a nice change of pace. I usually deal with people who are dead. Having a live one was...different," she sounded pleased with herself. As she should. She had saved him. That was good work. "Now we have to talk about you, Yonah."

"What about me?"

"You should really turn yourself in," Lily said, "Kris is breaking the law by not turning you in. They could arrest him for this."

"He knows I didn't do it. He also knows who did. He's afraid they'll try and murder me in custody, which they probably will since it's my sister and her asshole boyfriend who are behind all this."

"Your sister?"

"Yeah, she and Charles are trying to take over the world and put humans in their proper place. Humans are food to them. And only food. They want to reduce humans to cattle."

"That's terrible. We have to tell the Captain about this."

"Kris is trying to make it so that no one gets hurt. With the information he's gathered, he can probably back them off. He just needs to talk them around. Then again, seeing as they've taken a shot at him, he probably can't."

"Where is this information?" Lily asked. His voice was concerned, Kris could tell.

"I don't know. I don't know who he's told or where he has it hidden. He's probably trying to protect it. If he can't stop them, he'll hand it over; I'm sure."

Kris really didn't want that. He knew if he handed over that information, quite a few of his kind would be put away for crimes that had happened long ago but were crimes, nonetheless. Several creatures that were not vampires would go down as well. They were old friends, and even if they got out, they would never forgive him. He had to decide whether it was worth losing most of his friends. Even Ross might be in jeopardy if that information got out. *Damn*, he thought, *I don't know if I can do it.*

He kept listening. "You should still turn yourself in. We can protect you if you feel you're in danger, but Kris can't protect you. Not forever and certainly not now. He has to heal."

"I know. Some part of me just can't. I'm scared. I can admit that now."

"I know you are," she said, "but trust me, this is probably for the best."

Kris didn't want Zeke to do this. He could protect Zeke. He was the only one. "Lily!" he called out.

Lily and Zeke rushed into the room, "you alright?" She had that look on her face. Her concerned face.

Kris smiled, "I'm alright," he said, "I'm just pained."

"There's pretty much nothing I can do about that. You're not exactly human."

He laughed, "yeah, I know. Thank you for coming. I'm sorry you got dragged into this."

"Kris, you can't do this. It's far too dangerous for you on your own."

"It doesn't matter. I have to take care of him. There's no one else."

"That's not true, Kris. We can take care of him. Please, let me help. Let me take him in."

"Please," Kris said, "don't take him." He could barely hold on to consciousness. "I can't...what happened to me?"

"A bullet laced with dead man's blood. It isn't healing like it usually would.," Lily said, "You should rest, dear. Close your eyes, go to sleep. I'll take care of you in the morning."

"Thank you for coming," he said, only half awake, "I love you..." He fell into darkness then.

***

"Did he just say he loved me?" Lily asked.

Zeke was shocked as well. He hadn't heard those words come out of Kris's mouth in a long time. "Good lord..." Zeke didn't know what to make of it. He knew that Kris had feelings for her. He didn't know that they ran that deep. Or maybe it was just his current condition. "I'm not sure he actually meant it. He's kind of messed up right now."

"Yeah, I know. I pulled a damn bullet out of him."

"He'll be okay," Zeke said, "but what about me? You think I should go. That I should turn myself in?"

"The MLD is probably much more capable of taking care of you than Kris, especially now."

"You're probably right," he hated admitting it. As he stood over Kris, watching him sleep, he knew that she was right. "Take me in. It's best for all of us I think. But do not tell them that I know him."

"They'll probably find out anyway."

"Then I suppose it doesn't matter."

"No, come on. We'll take my car."

"He's not going to be happy when he wakes up in the morning, and I'm not here." Kris would blame her. He knew that he would. "I know it's not your fault. Let him know that."

"It's okay," she said, "I think he'll understand."

Zeke left with her. He wasn't sure he wanted to at first, but he had to do what was right for Kris. Even now, he would look out for the man he had once loved. Maybe he still did.

CHAPTER 7

Kris opened his eyes in the daylight and was almost blinded. "Damn light," he said as he rolled over, trying to avoid it. He winced as he rolled over on his wound, "dammit!" He heard footsteps rush into the room. He looked up from under his blankets. It was Lily standing there, "don't worry, I'm okay. Actually, I think it's almost healed."

"Yeah, that's why you're squealing and swearing," she said, smiling down at him.

He smiled back and sat up on the bed. He noticed that the mattress was still bloody under the sheet that they had draped over it. At least the sheet was clean. "Thanks again for coming."

"That's no problem, Kris."

Then he remembered something from last night that he thought might have been a dream but wasn't sure. He thought he would test out the theory that it was just a dream. "I had a dream last night," he said, "that I said I loved you. It was a dream, wasn't it?"

She nodded her head, "yeah, it was just a dream."

"I see," some part of him was a little disappointed. He had hoped that he had said it out loud and that she would have been happy to hear it. "It's okay. It was a good dream. Now, where is Zeke?"

The smile went from her face, "Zeke's not here."

Kris stood, though it hurt him to do so. "Where is he?"

"He's gone. He turned himself in last night."

"What?" Kris couldn't believe it. "Why?"

"He convinced himself that It was best for both of you."

"And I suppose you helped him come to this conclusion?"

"Kris, it was best for you both."

"I don't care! I have to check on him."

"Kris, you can't go out. You're still hurt." She tried to stop him. To stand in his way, but he was easily able to get by her with his vampire's speed. Once in his car, he made his way to the MLD office. Going to work that day was not a good idea. He walked in through the front door and, there were feren guards waiting for him. "What do you want?" He asked as they grabbed his arms.

"You are going to be questioned in connection with the investigation. We have Yonah, and he gave you up. Told us things. You're in a lot of trouble, my friend." This feren was Davey, who was usually a nice guy. Today, that wasn't the case, and Davey delivered Kris to Garner...in an interrogation room.

"Hello Kris," Garner said as he pointed to a pile of files on the table.

Damn, Kris said, *I should have hidden those.*

"Hello, Alexander. Having a nice day?"

"We found Yonah," Garner said, sitting across from Kris at the long, grey table. "He didn't tell us that you were the one who had been hiding him, but the feren found out regardless."

"Did you hurt him?"

"We're not torturers, Kris."

"I know the Feren's methods," Kris said, "they're not always as civil as we claim they are. Cracking minds is like stabbing someone to read their diary."

"We didn't hurt him. Then we searched your desk and found these. Files that show that there are multiple other crimes that he possibly was responsible for."

"Zeke didn't kill anyone, you asshole. I can prove it; I just need a bit more time."

"So, you do know the suspect?"

"Oh sure. He and I go way back. We used to hang out and lie in bed and talk."

"You would lie in bed and talk?"

"After other recreational activities, sure."

"You're gay?" Garner asked.

"Um no. You have noticed I have a thing for Lily, right? I'm bi, Garner. I love the gentlemen and the ladies."

"Yes, I noticed your thing for her." The dragon huffed a smoke ring and glared at him. "How unfortunate for you that she doesn't like pathetic losers."

Kris rolled his eyes, doing his best to restrain himself. This was not the time to try and get the last word. "So yeah, I know Zeke. Intimately."

"And why did you not disclose this information before?"

"Well, you know. Kissing and telling is just not classy."

Garner slammed his fist down on the table, "this is a murder investigation, goddammit!"

"Yes, you have a keen sense of the obvious. Would you like to point out something else that's painfully obvious? Like the walls are grey or you're a massive asshole?"

"My God, Kris. You could be arrested for this."

"Yeah, I know. Thanks for the update, Captain Obvious."

"What evidence do you have?" Garner's claws came out again, and he began to drum them on the table. Kris hated that. "You said you could prove his innocence. What do you have that we haven't found?"

"It's not what you haven't found. It's what only I know."

Garner's eyes blazed yellow, his fingers drumming more furiously. Kris smiled. He was getting under that scaly skin, and he loved it. Garner shook his head, "what the fuck does that even mean?!"

"That's for me to know and you to wonder."

Garner was about to go off again when the door opened and, Captain Harris came in. "Alexander, take a break, will ya?"

"Fine," Garner said, stalking out. *Victory*, Kris thought. It was a little immature. He was still proud of himself, though.

"Wipe that goofy-ass smile off your damn face," Harris said, "what the hell were you thinking? Hiding him; impeding the investigation."

"I had to," Kris said, "I look out for him. I used to love him."

"You used to love him?" She didn't seem to be amused by this.

"Yes, I loved him. What would you do for the people you love?"

"Oh, for goodness sake, Kris!" She shook her head, her wings quivered.

"I'm sorry, I fucked up. But something is starting within the vampire ranks. I can't say what just yet, but it's far bigger than any one murder."

"What?"

"I need more time."

"Well, you've got it. Consider yourself suspended until further notice." The frown on her face said everything. She was disappointed in him. For that he was sorry.

"I understand," Kris said, "just do me a favor and make sure that Zeke doesn't lose his head while he's in custody."

"I will do everything that I can to protect him."

"You have my thanks."

"Now get the hell out." She pointed at the door, refusing to look at him.

Kris left the MLD office and went back to his own apartment. It was the same place that it always had been, but he didn't feel as content with it as he had before. He sat down in his recliner and laid back. *Fucking Garner...*

There was a knock on the door. *How annoying.* He sat up and went to open it. Lily stood on the other side. "Hello there," he said, "I wasn't expecting to see you."

"I'm sorry. I heard what happened and I had to come see you. I thought you might still be in pain, and that's the least I could do for you."

"I'm alright," Kris said. He didn't know if he wanted to see her right now. She had thrown him under the bus. "I'm actually starting to heal. It's not as bad as it was last night."

"That's good, I just wanted to say that I was sorry for what happened."

"It's not your fault," Kris said, "I felt that I was the only one who could help him."

"I know. Is there anything I can do for you?"

"I don't think so."

"Well, I'm off today. Any chance you would want to go out for lunch?"

"I don't really eat," he said.

"I do, let's go."

At first, he was not sure how to respond to that, or if he even wanted to do it. He stepped out and closed the door behind him. "Sure, okay. Let's go."

They took her car to a restaurant that was not too far away. It was Mexican food, a little place called Alejandro's. He didn't really like Mexican food...or food in general, but at least he could have a beer. He sat across from her sipping his beer and watching her eat tamales. He had never had those before. "How do they taste?" He asked.

"Oh, pretty good," she said, "pork is always good."

"I've never had them before. I doubt they would have much taste, though."

"I'm sorry about that," she said, "I guess it's not cool just to eat in front of you."

"It's alright. You're human, you have to eat. I'm a vamp, If I'm going to hang out with you, I need to let you be human."

"That's good to know."

"You know, Zeke decided on his own that it would be best to turn himself in."

Kris frowned, "I don't really want to talk about that."

"Sorry, it's just..."

"As I said, I know it's not your fault. Zeke is five hundred ninety-five years old. He can make his own decisions. It's you youngins that I am concerned about."

"Kris, I'm thirty-nine. I'm not young."

"I'm five hundred seventy-two. Everyone is young to me. Even you, Lil. But what you did wasn't wrong. I don't even know if what I was doing was right."

"It was. It was misguided and ridiculous, but you were looking out for him. That's admirable."

"In a misguided and ridiculous kind of way, yeah, I guess."

He sipped off his beer. God he still loved to drink. Also, he took solace in the fact that he could still get drunk. "Are we going to make a day of this?"

"And do what?"

"I don't know. Have some fun, hang out, get hammered? I mean, I've got no place to be."

"Oh sure, where do you want to go?"

"Let's take a walk. Enjoy the day, walk under the sun?"

"Sure," she said, "anything you want."

Kris loved art. They ended up at the Glenbow Museum. The two of them walked the museum together, wandering through. They came across The Black Gold Tapestry by Sandra Sawatzky. It told a story through imagery, some of which was very familiar to Kris. The story of how oil had impacted history and civilization throughout time. Kris was five hundred years old and definitely knew how something like oil had affected mankind over the years. He looked at the people represented within their different time periods. He thought back to his youth and what things had been like when he was a young man, raising a family, being a husband. In some ways, it was a sadness to him. Though he had lived far longer than any human ever had or probably ever would; he couldn't help but remember everything he had to leave behind in the life he might have had if he had remained human. "It's beautiful," Kris said as he stared at it. "It brings back fond memories of the past."

"The past?" Lily asked.

"People don't exactly weave tapestries anymore."

"I guess you're right about that," she said.

He looked over at her, "Sometimes I wish that I had only had one lifetime. It would have been enough for me."

"I've heard this kind of thing before, but not from you."

"Sometimes I can't help but think it."

"You're not depressed, are you, Kris?"

"I'm not really happy," he said. He hadn't admitted that to anyone. Not in a long time anyway. "In five hundred years, a person witnesses far more human suffering than any one person should have to endure."

"And you're tired of it?"

"Yes, but there's nothing I can really do about it."

"What do you think would make you happy?"

"That's a silly question," he said. It was one he really didn't want to answer.

"Kris, I want to help you."

"How are you going to help me, eh?" It was an honest yet terrible question. "You can't help me. Unless you can give me death." Then he felt guilty, "I'm sorry, this conversation has gotten far too morbid. We should go."

"Yeah, I think so too."

They made their way out of the museum and over to Olympic Plaza. It was late in the day. A day that had started out so ugly was now pleasant and comfortable. They wandered through the park. Kris had taken Lily's arm as they wandered. "You're so warm," Kris said, "I don't usually feel warmth."

"You don't?"

"It's a vampire thing. We're dead, and death is cold. Want to watch the sunset?"

"Sure," she said.

They walked over to a bench and sat down together. As the sun went down, Lily rested her head on his shoulder, "you're a nice guy, Kris. This has been a good day. I know it didn't start out that way."

The sunset in a burst of orange and gold and then the stars started to peek out. "I have enjoyed our time. Could I interest you in dinner or a drink?"

"I like to drink."

"Do you? Let's go then."

They went to a restaurant that was not far from Kris's apartment. It was an Italian place this time around. Italian food was always a good idea. If it were spicy enough, he could still taste it. He ordered a spicy sausage dish and she ordered spaghetti. He tried to remember the taste of pasta and couldn't. "When I get home, I'm really going to need to have some blood," he said, "but I'm enjoying the meal for now."

"I've enjoyed our day together."

"So have I."

"But I have to ask, what's your problem with Alexander?"

"Oh, it's several things really. He's quite tall. I'm short and I hate it," she laughed, "He's handsome, but I'm not exactly model-esque, but I think it's because we both fancy you."

"Really?" She asked

He gave her a confused look. "Well, yeah. I would have thought that it was painfully obvious by now."

"For the most part, I just noticed the constant pissing contest going on."

"Well, it's true. Now that you know we both fancy you, what do you think?"

There was a jolt of pain in his side, he held it, grunting with the effort. "Damn, perhaps I'm not as healed as much as I thought I was."

"We'll go back to your place, and I'll take care of you."

"Thank you for that," Kris said. He smiled knowing that she would be coming back to his place. Then he realized that it probably wasn't a good idea. "Are you sure? It's late, and you probably need to get home. You work tomorrow, right? I can probably get it myself."

"Nonsense. I'll patch you up."

Damn...temptation. He had to be careful. The went back to his place and, in the bedroom, Lily checked his wound. He looked down at where the wound had been. It was beginning to heal. She carefully bandaged it again.

"It looks like it's almost as good as new."

"That's good," he said. It was weird having his shirt off in front of her. "Your hands are so warm. It's kind of weird that I can feel it."

She was so close, so warm and inviting. The temptation was almost too much. He leaned over and kissed her. After they parted, he looked into her eyes and there was no attraction to speak of. "Oh dear...I seem to have done wrong. Sorry...I'm such a dick."

"No, it's okay. That was my fault."

"So very sorry."

"I have to go."

"Yeah, that's probably best," he had messed up and he knew it. Or maybe she really wasn't interested. Either way, it was probably settled now. "I'll look after myself now, you don't have to come back."

"Kris, I..."

"Goodbye, Lily," He said as he laid back on the bed. She saw herself out. He laid there for some time, just staring at the ceiling. *Fucking erection...*

CHAPTER 8

The next morning, Kris didn't want to get out of bed. He knew that he had screwed up so badly that there was probably no coming back. His wound was almost healed, but he didn't want to get out of bed. He hid under the covers until ten o'clock. He'd botched things with Lily, he was sure of it. He shouldn't have tried to kiss her. He had cursed himself several times already. *How could you have been so stupid?* He had never wanted to die so much in his second life than he did now. *Please end me, God. I don't want to be here anymore.*

He didn't expect her, or anyone else to come around and visit him again. That's why he was so surprised when he heard the doorbell ring. He rolled out of bed and pulled his fluffy brown robe over his bare chest. He didn't think anyone would give a shit whether he was wearing pants. He just had to make sure that the thing didn't fly open. He slumped to the front door and threw it open.

"What?" He said, not even looking to see who it was.

"I'm happy to see you too," he heard Ross's voice. "Your dick is hanging out."

Kris looked down and confirmed that what Ross was saying was true. "And?" He said, and he shuffled away.

Ross followed him inside and shut the door. "I just thought you might want to put it away."

Kris threw himself down in the recliner and put it back. Ross was forced to avert his eyes as he sat down on the sofa, "please put that away."

Kris covered himself with the robe and eyed Ross leerily, "what do you want, Ross?"

"I heard you were suspended, and I thought I might come around and see how you were. I can see you're having a bad day."

"A bad day? A bad day? I am not having a bad day. I haven't been this depressed since my second life began. I have never wanted death more since that time."

"Oh my God, you're so dramatic," Ross said, rolling his eyes at the distressed vampire.

Kris glared at him, "You are such a creep! Then again, you never were Mr. Sensitive, were you?"

"I'm sorry if I sound insensitive," Ross said, "but you're five hundred years old. And far too old to let something like this get to you. You've lived for far too long to let losing your job defeat you."

"I also lost Lily. I did an asshole thing and I hate myself."

"I don't know who that is," Ross replied.

"She's the coroner with the MLD," Kris said, "I liked her, and I tried to kiss her. She rejected me. As for Garner, I don't really give a shit about him or what he would think."

"I'm sorry," Ross said. "You always were a romantic who fell hard and suffered hard."

"You would know," Kris scoffed. "You cheated on me."

"Yes, I know," Ross said, "I hurt you, and that was terrible of me. But if it makes you feel any better, I never got over you."

"I hope I haunt your dreams."

"You have in the past. And I don't expect you to forgive me. Ever. I'm literally the biggest dick in the world."

"Oh, stop it," Kris said, "I forgave you long ago. And I still love you. I blame Zeke for what happened, not you. He's a serial adulterer."

Ross was taken aback, "really?"

"Don't get me wrong. You're responsible for what you did. He's just slightly more responsible."

"So, you've forgiven me?" Ross asked.

"Yes, but you probably still shouldn't flatter yourself." Kris groaned, grabbing his side. "This thing still hurts."

"Is that where you were shot?"

"Yeah, it is."

"Do you need help?"

"I'll be okay. As for you, are you okay? I heard that Charles sent some people to talk to you."

"Yes, he did," Ross said, "which is part of why I'm not feeling as sympathetic as I usually would. Those dumbass vampires attacked me and beat me up trying to get the key you have me. It was okay though. I eventually got the drop on them. I was just pissed when I went to the box you told me to, and nothing was there."

"That's because I knew they were going to do what they did."

"So, you set me up?"

"Kinda, but you had it coming to you. Question: are you going to ask me out?"

Ross lifted an eyebrow in surprise. "You want to go out with me?"

"I'm not doing anything else."

"What if Charles's people attack us?"

"Let them come. We can take 'em."

"You sound brave."

Kris gave him a sly smile. "Yeah, Kinda."

***

Kris didn't go to movies. He certainly didn't enjoy the crappy action movies that Ross liked. He was happy to be with someone, though. He hadn't been out with Ross for a very long time, and he hadn't realized how much he missed the dragon. Even the dragon's strong serpentine scent was pleasant to him somehow. So, he sat through whatever lame action movie this was. He didn't know any of the people who were in it. They were all young and beautiful, but not very interesting.

Just for the fun of it, Kris reached his hand over on the armrest and touched Ross's, poking it with his pinky finger. Ross, with lightning reflexes, grabbed hold of Kris's hand and held it tight. Kris glanced over at the dragon who had a goofy grin on his face. Kris didn't take his hand back. He was enjoying the warmth. Ross was the one thing that could always warm him.

When they were through with the movie, which Kris didn't really enjoy, they went out for dinner. If there was one thing that Kris did like, it was Japanese food. He loved the burn of wasabi. As a vampire, he could eat a ton of it, enjoy the slight tingle it gave him, and then never have to worry about it again. Ross watched him eat. He had just finished eating a large platter of teriyaki chicken and was now waiting patiently. "You're so cute when you eat spicy things," Ross said.

"I can taste it," Kris said, "I've always been weird that way. Vampires aren't meant to be able to taste human food."

"I know, and it is odd, but you were always special."

"You mean different?" Kris asked.

"Different isn't bad," Ross said.

"I would like, just once, to be normal," Kris replied, "even in my human life I was unusual. I married old. My wife was twenty-five when we married. That was considered old back in the fourteen hundreds. We had one beautiful daughter and then we both died. Or at least, her mother died, and I was taken."

"By Charles?"

"He tied me to the foot of his throne and fed off me every day for almost a year."

Ross cocked his head, "that douchebag had a throne? Yeah, that sounds like the kind of douche thing he would do."

"He was going to keep me as his human, but then one of his vampires attacked me, and I couldn't be saved. Or at least my mortal life couldn't be. He should have let me die. I wished he would have. I could never go home again after that, nor could I stay with Charles and forgive him."

"You've told me this before, years ago when we first met."

"Yes, but I never told you the worse part."

"Which was?"

"He told me that he loved me; that we were meant to be together, and there would be no other for me," Kris swallowed hard. He didn't like to talk about it. "Ever since then, every lover I've ever been with has cheated on me. I couldn't help but wonder whether he was right. That the only person I could ever be with is him. I don't love him, and I don't want to be with him. But would that mean that I can't have anyone?"

Ross lifted an eyebrow in confusion. "Are you suggesting that you think you're cursed? Because vampires don't do that. They don't have that kind of magic."

"But they know people who do," Kris said, taking a drink from his cup of tea.

"Oh sure, Kris. Charles is such a nice guy that he has witches clambering to do him favors." Ross rolled his eyes.

"Well, you never know. Witches will do anything if you pay them enough. They're all mercenaries. Almost as bad as the feren."

"Trust me, you're not cursed, you've just run into a few assholes. I'll freely admit that I'm one of them." Ross said. "In fact, I'm surprised that you wanted to go out with me. I hurt us both with my actions in the past."

'I forgave you," Kris reminded him.

"You shouldn't have," Ross hung his head, "You were perfect. How could I have cheated on you?"

"Because you're an idiot. But you're an idiot that I still love, and I'm willing to give you another chance."

"I don't deserve it."

"Yes, I know you don't," Kris said, "now please shut up before you ruin everything."

Ross laughed. "You know me too well."

"Yes, I do. Are you ready to go back to my place? I think I need help with my bandages."

Ross gave him a devilish grin, "I'll have to bind you up really tight."

"I would expect no less from such a powerful dragon," Kris said. He probably shouldn't be trying to start a relationship with the dragon so quickly. But right now, there was just one thing that he really wanted. He wanted Ross, and he was going to have him, in his bed, with the kind of fun he used to enjoy with Zeke. "C'mon. You're paying right?"

"Yeah, apparently I am."

***

Things heated up at Kris's house almost immediately as he sat down on the bed and stripped off his shirt to reveal his bandages. Ross stood over him as he pulled the bandages away from the wound. It was nearly healed but was still red and irritated. Ross knelt by Kris's side and looked at the red mark, reaching a finger up and drawing it lightly over the spot.

A smile crossed Kris's face, the warmth felt *so* good. "You're so hot." Ross looked up at him. Kris moved in for a kiss. He hadn't expected things to be this wonderful, this quickly. He knew that he had never really gotten over

Ross, but to want him this badly so soon. He fed off his lover's lips, giggling happily as he did so. He reached down and grabbed Ross around the waist and pulled him up onto the bed. "I want you to be hot inside of me," Kris said.

Ross lifted an eyebrow, a little surprised by Kris's words. "You want me to…?"

"Don't think about it too hard, love. Just take me," Kris kissed him again. It wasn't long before Ross did just that, and Kris was lost to him again.

***

Hours later, Kris laid on his side with Ross tightly curled against his back. Every inch of him was hot. It was even hotter when it was inside him. Fire breathing dragons were toastier than most other dragons. Humans had a difficult time making love to them because dragons sometimes burned their lovers when they got too excited. They had to be very careful.

The dragon was purring happily in his ear. It was a comfort to feel the vibrations against his skin. "I've missed you so," Kris told him.

"And I you."

"Do you think we could do this again? Have a relationship?"

The purring in his ear stopped. "Is that what you want?"

"I should know," Kris gave a sigh, "but I remember how terrible it was when you cheated on me."

"Something I'll never do again."

"I can't be sure of that," Kris lamented.

"Would you like if you could?"

"How could you make me that promise? Didn't you make a similar promise before?"

"I hadn't claimed you. Dragons don't usually do that. And after what you told me about Charles, I was not sure if I should even mention it."

"I've never heard of it."

"As I said, dragons don't usually do that. When they do, it means they'll never take another lover. As long as you live, I will be yours."

Kris rolled over and looked deeply into his love's eyes, "I don't want that for us. I want you to love me and be with me because you want to. Not because of some dragon bullshit that says you can't be with someone else."

"Alright, but I thought I would mention it."

"We should just try and make this work instead. You make me happy. Let's just leave it at that for now."

Ross smiled wistfully at his love. "You make me happy too. We'll make it work." Ross wrapped his arms around Kris, and the vampire buried his face in the dragon's shoulder. He wanted this to work. He wanted to be happy with Ross. He just hoped that Charles and his insanity wouldn't get in the way.

CHAPTER 9

Kris woke up early the next morning and found the dragon still fast asleep in his bed. He was beautiful and peaceful when he slept. He stroked his lover's cheek as he slept. Then he rose, dressed, re-bandaged and was out the door. He had left a note on the kitchen counter, hoping that Ross wouldn't worry when he woke and found Kris gone.

Kris was on a mission. He was going to go to the MLD and see how Zeke was doing. He was pretty sure that they were doing their best to take care of him while in custody. Lily would make sure of that. He just wanted to see for himself. He also wanted to go to Charles's club to see if he could get a word again with Charles. He knew it was probably a bad idea, and that he had been suspended. He just wanted the vampire to stay nervous and know that he was still watching. "I know what you did in Aberdeen was always a powerful threat. Charles's rampage of terror with his vamp clan took out a good many good Scottish people that night. Kris never wanted to see that again.

Kris was walking to his car when he was grabbed from behind and something thin, but firm was wrapped around his neck. It was a silver chain and smoke began to rise from where the silver touched bare skin. Silver didn't affect vampires as terribly as it affected werewolves, but it still sapped his strength. It also burned, but it didn't seem to burn Kris as badly as other vampires. It didn't cause the flash-burn type wounds that most other vampires got when they were exposed to silver. He tried to turn and fight as he was seized by men who bound his hands behind him with another silver chain, placing a hood over his head and shoving him into the trunk of a car. He hated car trunks! This wasn't his first time he'd been in one, and it probably wouldn't be his last. He wasn't strong enough to break free. His wound was beginning to hurt again. *Fucking silver.*

It seemed like his journey in the trunk took forever. The lid was opened, and he was hoisted out. Kris cried out as his wound opened up again. He was then taken by both arms and escorted across a gravel driveway. He knew it was gravel because it crunched under his feet. Kris could also hear bird song and the wind rustling the branches in a nearby tree. The vampire was hauled up some stairs into a house. Then, after a short trip down a wooden hall, he was hauled down more stairs into a darkened room. It had to be a basement or cellar.

He was then thrust against a cold, stone wall and was bound to it with the chains that bound him. Kris squirmed, finally getting to his knees. His arms trembled from both fear and the effects of the silver. The hood was removed, and he came face-to-face with someone he didn't know. A tall man with long, black wavy hair and a youthful, gorgeous face, Kris couldn't help his fascination with the handsome man. The man who had vamp-napped him for reasons he obviously couldn't understand. Was he a hunter or slayer? He just stood there in his well-tailored black suit and smiled like an angel.

"Who are you?" Kris glared at the man.

The handsome man observed him for a moment and then turned to the thugs who were obviously the vampire-nappers and were now standing on either side of the stranger. "The vampire is bleeding. Did you damage him?"

One of the thugs looked down at him, and Kris looked down at his shirt. He was bleeding alright. The stain was large and growing. "We didn't do that," the man assured him.

"You bastards," Kris's teeth were gritted in anger and pain. "It was healing."

"What did this to you?" The handsome man had a curious look on his face.

"A bullet," Kris wanted to hold his wound. To stop the bleeding. He doubted he would bleed out. It was still uncomfortable, though. "Laced in dead man's blood."

"I'm impressed. I have never seen anything like it before. Hunters?"

"No, other vamps. Now, you know what I am. Who the fuck are you and why did you vampire-nap me?"

The man raised an eyebrow, "are you afraid of me?"

"Does it matter?"

"No, not really. As for who I am, I am Alejandro Valdez. I am a member of a very old organization known as *The Watchers*. Our job is to watch out for special people like you. The MLD is good at what they do, but they haven't even caught on to us or what we do. They miss things when it comes to magical crime, and that's where we come in."

"What?" Kris shook his head in disbelief. "Are you magical?"

"Not at all," Alejandro smiled, "we're human. We just don't want to see creatures like you go extinct. And believe me, if Charles Anderson keeps going in the direction that he's going, that will happen."

"I know it's bad," Kris said. "He's murdered a few people and has made some others disappear. But I'm sure that's the extent of it."

Alejandro rolled his eyes with disdain. "You fool. It goes far deeper. He's selling people by the hundreds. I'm not sure, but in the states, there might even be children involved."

"Children?" Kris was shocked.

"Young-blood is good for the vamp's soul."

"Vamps don't have souls," Kris reminded him.

"That doesn't matter. The fact is, he's trading in living blood, and that puts all magical creatures at risk."

"Yes, it does," Kris was shocked. There were things that they seemed to know that none of the rest of them knew. "What can we do?"

"I don't know, but there are new bands of hunters and slayers forming, especially in the United States and they already suspect things."

"I have information on the vamps. A huge file on Charles."

"We already know enough about Mr. Anderson. We need new information. To find out not only who he's selling the humans to and how, but where he's keeping the vampires that he's making disappear."

Kris shook his head, "I don't know if I can. Charles already knows that I'm out to get him."

"Then you have to try harder."

"That's easy to say."

"Mr. Kellman, we need to know. He's made hundreds of his own disappear."

"I didn't know that he was taking out so many vampires."

"He may also be after your dragon friend. Right now, he's barely tolerating him. If he wanted the dragon dead, he would make it happen."

"Dammit," Kris said, "I'll try and find out what you need. But if he gets to me first..."

"I know," the man replied, "however, we have to try."

Kris nodded. The thugs then placed the hood back over his head and carried him out the same way that they carried him in. When they pulled up in front of his apartment building, they released him from his chains and threw him out into the street. Then they left him there. Kris laid him there for a moment, his head still swimming. He had to do something. He just didn't know what. His maker had made a mess of things. Now it was his job to clean it up.

***

Kris was finally able to get up. He limped into the apartment building and nearly collapsed onto the floor as he was opening the door. Ross was there to catch him though. Dragons could move very quickly when they wanted to. Crossing from the kitchen to the doorway took mere seconds. He held Kris in his arms. "Where the hell have you been? What's happened?" Kris saw Ross look down at the blood on his shirt. "Kris, my God. You're bleeding."

"Yes, and I need blood. Can you carry me to the bedroom?"

"Yes," Ross carefully picked Kris up in his arms and carried him into the bedroom. He sat Kris down on the bed and ran to the kitchen to get him some blood. Kris carefully slipped his shirt off and looked down at the wound. The bleeding had stopped, but the wound looked angry again. He laid back on the bed. Staring up at the ceiling, Kris thought back to the time in his life when he could have still died from a wound like this. It was long ago, but now that he was reminded of what mortality was like, the memories felt fresh.

Ross rushed back into the room with a glass filled with blood. He helped Kris to sit up, putting the rim of the glass to his lips. Kris drank deeply, and he felt better. He laid back again, having finished the blood. "I think I'll live."

"What the fuck happened to you?" Ross asked. "You disappeared this morning, were gone all day without a word, and come back like this?"

"I was kidnapped."

"By who? By Charles?" Ross sounded as if he were about to have a heart attack.

"Calm down," Kris murmured, "I'm alright. I was kidnapped by a group known as The Watchers. They said they're humans who look out for creatures like us."

"That doesn't make any fucking sense, Kris. Why would any human want to help monsters like us?"

"Because we aren't monsters. We're just another endangered species, and these are animal conservationists."

"That is…really insulting." Ross sounded disgusted. Kris stared at the ceiling again.

"Maybe it is. Maybe it's just the damn truth."

"What did they want?" Ross just sounded angry now.

"They're worried about Charles. That what he's doing could get us all killed, and we'll go from being endangered to being extinct."

"Or are they worried that what he's doing might work and they'll end up on the bottom of the food chain?"

"Does it matter? The fact is, they're right. This isn't going to end well for beings like us. This is more serious than I thought. It's not just a few murders or people disappearing. It's not just a few vampires that are disappearing either. The conspiracy goes further than I thought."

Ross laid down next to him. "That's annoying. Everything is annoying now."

"Tell me about it. People keep kidnapping me."

"You mean vamp-napping?"

"You really want to quibble about terms now?"

The dragon chuckled, "No, not really. What do we do about this?"

"I could go to the MLD about this."

"What about the Vampire Council?"

"In Montreal? Chances are, if the conspiracy truly goes this deep, then they're probably in on it. I can't trust my brethren. I'm the enemy now."

"Are you saying Charles owns them?"

"What other conclusions can I come to considering the information I've been given. There's no way they don't know about it. If they truly wanted to stop this, they would have done so by now."

"They told me that I need evidence for the MLD so that they can step in and go after Charles."

Ross rolled over onto his side and stared intently at Kris. Kris could sense his trepidation, so he rolled over and gave his lover a reassuring look.

"Don't give me that look. You know this is dangerous. You should let me claim you. That way I can always feel your life force. Or your unlife force…whatever. You still have a soul, and I would still be able to sense it."

"That's not possible," Kris lamented. "Vampires don't have souls."

"I'm not so sure about that. There's something different about you. I've always been able to feel it in you."

"I still don't want you to do that. Besides, Charles is my maker. If anything, he's already claimed me."

"Intimately?"

Kris moaned. "No, thank God."

"He's really hot, you know," Ross laughed.

"If he touches me, I'll scream."

"Yeah, I know," The dragon reached over and stroked Kris's cheek. "I just got you back. I can't lose you."

"You won't," Kris said, but he knew it was a promise he might not be able to keep. Charles was tricky and had many mercenaries and assassins at his disposal. The one he had already faced had been a pro. He leaned over and kissed his lover. "I'll be alright." He whispered as they parted. He hoped, beyond hope, that he was right.

CHAPTER 10

The next day, Kris did what he had intended to do the morning before and drove to the MLD offices, intent on seeing Zeke. At first, security didn't want to let him in. Captain Harris intervened on his behalf and walked with him down to the cells in the basement. On the way, she felt it was best they have a conversation. "How have you been, Kris?" She asked.

"I'll live," He replied, "I always seem do."

"A fairy lawyer named Tim Dent delved into Yonah's mind. He found memories from the night of the murder. Memories that we hadn't found before."

Kris stopped in his tracks, "Zeke approved this probe? He hates fairies, and he certainly doesn't enjoy being mind-fucked by them."

"Lily talked him into it. At first, he was reluctant, but she convinced him that it was best."

"Goddammit," Kris mumbled, "I knew this would happen. That's why I didn't want him to come here. He hates that sort of thing. He was once kidnapped by feren who tried to sell him to slayers. Those fairy assholes tortured him. Went into his mind, made him see and feel things that weren't really happening, but sure felt like they were." He started to walk again, "you shouldn't have put him through that."

"We didn't know," Alison replied.

"He doesn't like to talk about it," Kris huffed, "he doesn't like to be reminded of that pain."

"Well, we got to the truth," she said.

"Sure, you did," Kris's words dripped with sarcasm, "but at what price? Re-victimizing a victim is never the right way to go."

"We didn't know," She cried, "how are we supposed to know things if he doesn't tell us?"

"It doesn't matter now. What's done is done. Just take me to him."

She took him to an interview room. Zeke sat at the table, staring at the grey wall. He didn't even look up when Kris entered. Or even when he sat down across from him. "Zeke," Kris said, trying to get the other vampire's attention. "They told me what happened. I'm so sorry."

"It's not your fault," Zeke said. "They wouldn't have known. And at least now they know that it wasn't me. They're going to arrest her, Kris. They're going to arrest Anna."

"I know," Kris reached a hand across the table, and Zeke reached over and took it. "I'm sorry. I know that she's family, but this is for the best."

"They still won't let me go, Kris. They said that they're keeping me here for my own good. I don't want to be here anymore. Can you help me?"

Kris shook his head, "sadly no. You just have to hold out for a bit longer. Just let me try and get Charles and then we can all go home."

"Charles, he's a slippery devil."

"And his crimes go far deeper than I had feared. There are far more people involved than we originally thought, and it may go all the way to The Vampire Council. I've been asked to find more information."

"More information? What information? Who's asking?"

"I can't tell you, but I can say that, if I should disappear, you'll be safe here. Trust Harris. She's a good fairy. As for Lily, I'm a little surprised that she forced you to undergo a mind probe."

"It's alright, Kris," Zeke reassured him, "she's been good to me, and there's no way she could have known. But if you're truly terrified for your life, maybe you should talk to someone here. Get the MLD involved."

"I would," Kris said, "but I think this is something that I have to attempt by myself."

Zeke rose from his chair. Kris got up and embraced his old friend and former lover. "Find Ross if anything happens to me," he whispered into Zeke's ear. Then he left Zeke behind. Out in the hall on the way out of the basement, Kris ran into Garner who looked unhappy about something. He grabbed Kris's shoulder as he passed by. "What do you know about this that we don't? Who's asking you to gather information?"

Kris pulled his arm out of the dragon's grasp. "That's none of your fucking business."

"You're still facing possible arrest. If you have any information for us, I suggest you spill it."

"I'm not telling you a Goddamn thing." Kris glared at the dragon, "now, fuck off, you eavesdropping asshole."

Garner grabbed his arm again and slammed him back against the wall behind them, pressing him hard against it. Kris struggled against him. "Tell me what you know," the dragon hissed, blowing smoke into Kris's face.

Kris finally succeeded in pushing him away and ran up the stairs. He rushed out of the building, trying to get to his car as quickly as possible. He wasn't sorry that he had come, but he didn't want to stick around if Garner was going to go on a rampage.

***

When Ross got back to Kris's apartment after work, he found that vampire lying back in his recliner and sipping blood from a wine glass. Kris had a satisfied look on his face. It was almost happy. "Good evening, love," Kris gave him a devilish smile.

"What are you so happy about?" Ross asked, amused by the vampire's good mood.

"Zeke is off the hook. They're going to arrest and charge his sister with the murder."

"And what about you? Did they give you your job back?" Zeke came over and sat down on the sofa.

"Nah," Kris swirled his glass, the blood was thick inside of it, coating the sides, "I was thinking maybe I would become a private investigator instead."

"That's a good idea," Ross replied, "you have the skills for it."

"Well, yeah. They just have to officially fire me."

"Is that what you want?"

Kris thought about it for a moment. He wasn't sure, Ross could tell from the look on his face that he wasn't. "I'm pretty sure, yeah." Kris was lying to him, but he would give it a pass. Right now, the vampire was happy, and that didn't happen very often.

"So, what do you want to do?" Ross asked.

Kris sat up in the recliner and got to his feet. He put the glass down on the coffee table and bent down to kiss Ross hard on the lips. Ross was a little surprised by the vampire's ferocity. "Well, my goodness, aren't you feisty," he murmured between kisses.

"C'mon," Kris straddled him, "you know that's what you love about me."

Ross shrugged, "sure, but are you sure that you want to fuck on the sofa?"

The vampire looked at him in confusion, "the sofa? I'm about to give you the ride of your life, and you're worried about the upholstery?"

"Kris, someone as OCD as you wouldn't want to stain the sofa."

"What?" Kris sounded annoyed, "why does everyone keep saying I have OCD? I don't have OCD."

"There's the vamp I know and love," Ross chuckled, "but seriously?"

"You're right, I don't want to stain the sofa."

"Then shall we go to the bedroom?"

"Carry me?"

"Oh c'mon…" Ross rolled his eyes.

"Please?" Kris gave him adorable doe eyes. Ross couldn't resist it when Kris gave him doe eyes. He got to his feet and swept the vampire off his feet. Kris giggled giddily. "I knew I could make you do it."

"You're so crazy. I love that about you."

"Let's go then. I need you in me now."

"So demanding."

"Stop talking and take me to the bed, you daft cretin!"

"As you command, my love."

Ross carried Kris into the bedroom and placed him gently on the bed. The vampire gave him a coy smile, "such a gentleman."

"I aim to please," the dragon said as he stripped off his leather jacket and threw it into onto a nearby chair.

"Oh my," Kris said, "keep going, I'm not quite pleased yet."

The vampire watched with a wicked smile as the dragon stripped in front of him. He was perfect. This was a body that most men would kill for, Kris lifted his eyebrows, "my goodness, I wish I were half as impressive."

Ross, who was down to his boxers, pounced on his lover, his hands at the collar of Kris's shirt. He ripped it open and looked down admiringly at what he saw. "I'm impressed, are you ready to impress me further?"

"You ripped my shirt," Kris said dourly.

"That's not the only fabric that's going to be ripping tonight."

"Wow, you haven't been this excited since nineteen forty-two when we had sex in that bomb shelter as the bombs fell on London."

"This is not the time for nostalgia," Ross ripped open Kris's trousers. "Oh, I am quite impressed. We're going to need a lot of lube and probably a condom."

"Top drawer of the nightstand," Kris sat up and pulled off what was left of his shredded shirt. Ross opened the drawer of the nightstand and found what he needed. When he turned back, Kris was lounging on his side, his head propped up on his hand, a goofy look on his face and his cock hard between his legs. One leg was arched up, his foot resting on his knee. "Are you ready, love?"

"Oh, God yes," Ross murmured.

***

"I love you," Ross said that night after the lovemaking session. "I could claim you," Ross said. "I could make you my mate forever."

Kris didn't want to think about that right now, "Not tonight, my love."

Ross kissed him and laid down by his side. "I'm sorry, Kris. I just don't want to lose you."

"You won't, my love," Kris wrapped his arms around the dragon. He held his love close. He wanted that warmth to be by his side forever, but he didn't want any magic influencing their love, no matter what it was.

***

The next morning, as Kris slept with his love wrapped around him, he heard his phone ring. He picked it up off the nightstand and looked to see who it was. Alison's name came up on the caller ID. He answered it. "Let me guess, I'm fired."

"I'm sorry, Kris," He could hear the sadness in her voice. "We just couldn't overlook the fact that you harbored a suspect and hid vital information from us. We've been able to link all the murder cases that you tried to hide from us to Anna Yonah, but that doesn't change anything."

"And you didn't even want to bring me in and talk to me about this?" He questioned. He didn't seem to be getting a fair chance to speak for himself.

"You're actually lucky. We could have had you arrested and brought charges."

"Fine then," he said, "It's been good working with you." He ended the call. Kris was so sick of this nonsense. He threw the phone across the room and heard a loud cracking sound as it hit the wall. He then curled into his dragon again and tried to go back to sleep. Ross shifted.

"You've been sacked, haven't you?"

"Yup," Kris replied, turning over to look into Ross's eyes. "I think I'll go back to being a PI."

"You're still going after Charles though. And there will be no one to watch your back. The MLD offered you a little protection."

"I don't need them," Kris cuddled into Ross's chest. "I have you." He was soon asleep again in his lover's arms.

CHAPTER 11

K ris didn't need the bandages anymore. He was almost completely healed now. He could feel the wound on the inside was also almost completely healed. *I messed up last night.* Or at least that's what he kept telling himself. Today he was going to go see Charles and see if he knew where Anna was. He was sure that if he were able to bring her in himself, he would probably be able to get his job back. He put on a simple button-down blue shirt and jeans. Who was he trying to impress? No one obviously. He remembered then that he didn't have a phone. He'd thrown his against the wall. Something else that he had to take care of today.

He went to his car. He was so hoping that today things would just go as they were supposed to. Nothing seemed to be going well. He needed a win. He drove. The club would probably be empty this early in the morning. He was halfway there when he noticed that someone may be following. He kept his eye on the rear-view mirror. The car followed him for several blocks and then turned off. Maybe they weren't tailing him.

He was only a few blocks away when the car that he thought had been tailing him plowed into him at full speed. His car flipped and came to rest against a lamppost nearby. Glass shattered and metal crumpled and cracked. Is was like smashing a beer can times a thousand. Luckily it was just him and the lamp post, and grass. He crawled out of the window of the upside-down car, he was bleeding and pained again. There were shards of glass stuck in his arms and face and a jagged metal fragment stuck in his leg. The wounds would heal, but that did little to ease the pain right now. Dammit, his luck was wretched of late. Especially when someone grabbed him from behind and plunged a needle into his neck. His arms were pulled back to the point of breaking. This was another vampire. Long, dark hair fell over his shoulder, and he was pretty sure that he knew who it was. She wasn't there to kill him. That was boring. He could smell it; dead man's blood. *Fucking dead blood,* he thought right before he passed out.

He didn't expect to wake up. When he did, he was in the chair. He couldn't pull free. *Fucking chair.*

CHAPTER 12

Kris woke. His eyes were bleary, and he didn't know where he was, or what this was all about, but it was freaking him out. He was handcuffed to a large metal chair that was bolted to the floor. His right arm hurt like hell. Someone had injected him with something recently. His eyes strained to make out any shape in the stygian blackness, but there didn't seem to be anything else in there anyway. Kris could only see the light when he looked up toward the ceiling. *Skylights? Where the hell am I?*

He struggled, but he was weak and was unable to break free. He was stuck until someone chose to set him free. He heard someone come into the room. The way that the footsteps were echoing when they hit the floor made him think that this was a large building. Maybe an empty warehouse or something? He could also tell that whoever this was, it was probably a woman. The sound he heard was the clacking of heels. *A woman?* He thought he knew who it might be. When the footsteps grew closer, he asked the obvious question. "Anna, where the hell am I and what are you doing?"

"You're in a building that Charles owns. You remember Charles, right?"

"The vampire you cheated on me with? Who could forget? He kidnapped me the other day. Fucking asshole." Kris said, annoyed. "You kidnapped me, Why? You know that the magic police will come looking for me."

"The Magical Law Division? They may come, but they will come too late," she said.

"You set up your brother."

"I had to. He was in the way. He would have tried to stop Charles and me. We're on a mission, Kris. For vampires to take their proper place in the world."

"As gods who feed upon the innocent," Kris said, "I do know what you're up to. You plan on making humans nothing more than cattle to slaughter. You've been trafficking people as blood slaves, and I have no idea what you've been doing with those kids you've been stealing."

"That's what they're there for. To be food, not friends, not lovers, not equals. They're only good for food. You have no other choice, Kris. You're our prisoner now and your veins now flow with dead man's blood. Join your brethren, your vampire brothers and sisters. Do this or Charles will have you boxed and knotted."

"How very old school of you. You're going to bury me alive with a bunch of magical knots that will take a thousand years each to undo. That's illegal," Kris said, "It's cruel and unusual even among our own kind. Would you truly do something so cruel and torturous? If you do this, it will kill me. I'm weak with this poison you're pumping into me. Is that what you want for me? For your brother? You set him up for a murder he didn't commit!"

Kris fell back in the chair. He was lightheaded and nauseated.

"I no longer care what happens to you or Zeke. You stand in our way. You're both weak."

"Please, I beg of you. Don't do this! I mean, you and I, we used to love each other, right?"

She rolled her eyes, letting Kris know that she wasn't interested reminiscing. "That was a long time ago, Kris. I remember a time when you used to fill me with desire, but those days are gone."

He knew she was done with him. "I can't remember any time when it was good for me. You were always a frigid bitch."

"We all knew that you liked Zeke better."

"You will be murdering one of your own in you have me knotted. Please, stop this before it's too late. Charles is going to start a war with the humans. Is that what you really want. Please, don't do this."

"Then do the smart thing, and maybe Charles will show you mercy. Until then," she took a syringe out of the purse she carried with her. It was full of dark, coagulated blood. The needle was huge with a large opening at the tip. She grabbed his arm and jammed the needle into Kris's arm. He cried out when the blood entered his vein.

"Goddamn, you!" He seethed.

"Think about it," she said, "Charles will be back in a couple of days. Then, your time will be up."

She walked away and left Kris alone. He did everything he could to keep from vomiting, but in the end, he couldn't help himself. The front of his shirt was covered in blood. He was never going to get that stain out. *Fucking stain...*

He wasn't strong enough to escape. Yet another thing that pissed him off to no end. He also hated the fact that he now had to get rid of one of his favorite shirts because he had vomited blood all over it. He'd liked his blue shirt. It brought out the color of his hazel eyes. He had tried so desperately to pull free. His wrists were a bloody, shredded mess. Sadly, it was no use. He could have called for help, but he was pretty sure it was no use. He hadn't heard another sound outside since Anna had left. No cars or other vehicles. This place was isolated. There was no one to hear him. He was left on his own with nothing but his thoughts. He hated his thoughts!

He was left alone for two days. He watched the sunlight come in through the windows and then disappear. He was starving. He needed blood. He didn't know how long he could go without, but he was sure it wasn't much longer. Especially with the poison running through his veins.

He waited, and Anna finally came back with a thermos full of blood for him. It was a clear bottle. He could see it, and it was driving him mad with want. He pulled even more fiercely on his bonds. As she approached, she slapped him hard across the face. "Settle down." He didn't want to. His fangs descended, and he hissed loudly at her. She slapped him again. "I said to calm the fuck down!"

There was no choice. He was starving, but he wasn't going to get what he wanted until he calmed himself. He forced himself to do so, sitting back in the chair. She opened the lid and helped him to drink, putting the spout to his lips. He drank greedily. When it was gone, he was still desperate. It wasn't enough. At least not for a full belly. "More," he said, "I need more."

"No more for you," she said, "or at least not until tomorrow."

"Where is Charles?" He asked. Charles was the one who had ordered this. "He had better show up and let me go. And when he does, I will fucking kill him!"

"I don't think so, dear. Charles is away on business. He'll be back in a few days."

"Business? What business is that, being an asshole?"

"A financial thing in London that doesn't concern you."

"Being a money-grubbing asshole? Got it."

"You are a glutton for punishment," Anna glared at him. "If you don't behave, I will have to hurt you."

"You're going to hurt a bound man who can't fight back?"

"I'm a bitch that way. Now stay here and be a good boy. I'll be back tomorrow."

"Hey, bitch!" He spits in her face.

He knew he shouldn't have done that as she wiped it away. She slapped him again. "You are a naughty, naughty boy, and now you have to be punished." She took off a flowered scarf that she was wearing and shoved it into his mouth and then wrapped the rest of it around his head, tying it tightly. A gag was unnecessary, but it would be annoying. "I won't be coming back tomorrow," she said, "you've earned yourself some solitude."

No! He hadn't had enough food. He was starving. A whole day without would be almost unbearable. He cried behind the gag.

"You brought this on yourself," She said and then she walked away from him. She was going to kill him. *Fucking bitch!*

CHAPTER 13

Kris was gone, and Ross was worried about him. While he wasn't the vampire's keeper and he knew that sometimes vampires like to go off on their own, especially when they were hunting, he was still worried. Charles's people were watching him. He knew that now. They were watching him at his job at the club. They were following him when he went home. They were watching his place and Kris's. Something had happened to the vampire; he knew it.

He knew that Kris had friends at the MLD. He knew the name of at least one. Lily. Kris had loved her. He had told Ross that he had a thing for her. That he had lost her. Now, Kris was lost, and he was hoping that he could at least ask her if she had seen him. He had picked up Kris's phone after he had tossed it after being fired. It was broken, but Ross was hoping he could at least access the address contacts.

He went to the kitchen where he'd left the phone on the counter. The screen was cracked as hell, but when he pressed the power button, it lit up. He tried to open it hoping that it wasn't password protected. He got lucky.

Kris hated complicated things, and a million different passwords just weren't his style. He went into the contacts and found Lily's number. Ross got out his own phone and dialed the number.

There was no answer, and he decided to leave a voice message. "Hello, this is Ross Harris. I'm Kris's boyfriend." Ross hated using that term, but it was the best way to describe their relationship. "Kris has gone missing, and I was just wondering if you had any idea where he might be? Please, if you could call me back, I would appreciate it." He gave her his phone number and then ended the call. He didn't expect to hear from her. Ross knew he had to find Charles. The vampire wouldn't tell him anything, but he had to confront him.

A few days later Charles came into the club. Ross took that opportunity to speak with him. He pulled Charles aside and took him over to a booth. He sat down across from the vampire. He got right to it. "I don't appreciate you sending your goons to spy on my boyfriend and me."

"Your boyfriend? And who would that be?"

"You know who it is. You've been watching our places for days. Where's Kris Kellman?"

"Damned if I know," Charles said nonchalantly. "It's not like I'm his keeper. Or at least I'm not anymore."

"You're lying to me, vamp slime." Ross huffed smoke out of his nose into Charles's face. "You took him, didn't you?"

"He was in the way, just like the others. It's unfortunate. He was beautiful. I'm a little envious that you know him intimately and I don't."

"But you do have him, you have at least admitted that."

"Yes, you caught me in an admission. Good for you."

"Are you going to kill him?" Ross asked, "I could tell the MLD that you're keeping one of their people a prisoner."

"Oh, you could. However, you have no evidence to back that assertion up."

That devious bastard. He was right. Ross had to do something. "Tell me where he is, or I will bring dragon fire down upon your house and your people."

"A threat?" Charles gave him a sly smile, "I could report you for making such threats."

"Oh, I suppose you could."

"Also, you're fired."

"That's the way you want to play it?"

"Yes, that's the way this is going to happen. Come back here, and I will report you; if I don't bury you."

"You're going to kill me?" Ross began to laugh hysterically, "I'd like to see you try."

"Believe me, I can do that. Now get out."

Ross glared at Charles for a moment. "You haven't won."

"Actually, for the moment I have. By the way, I plan to deal with Kris soon."

Ross had no choice. He had to leave. He made the decision then and there that he was going to go to Charles's property and seek out Kris there. He would probably get himself killed, but he had to save Kris. Somehow...

***

Ross went back to Kris's place that night. The vamps were still watching it. He wished that he could take care of them, but they would have to make the first move for it to be self-defense. He nodded to them as they waited outside in their car. They glared back at him. He gave them the finger. He had just walked into the apartment when his phone vibrated in his jacket pocket. He pulled it out. "Hello?"

"Hello, this is Lily. You called me a couple of days ago about Kris going missing."

94

"Yeah, I did. I didn't expect you to call back," He was a little baffled that he was hearing from her. "Interesting that you waited for two days to get back to me."

"I don't know you. I had to make sure that you were who you said you were. Kris's friend Zeke said that you're a good guy. He was surprised that you and Kris got back together."

Ross smiled, "was he?"

"So, how long has Kris been missing?"

"For three days. I'm sure that he was going to try and confront Charles Anderson about Anna Yonah."

"Why would he do that? He's not with the MLD anymore."

"I think he still feels compelled to deal with Yonah and Anderson. They're involved in bad business, and Kris has personal issues with Anderson. He was the vampire who turned Kris. Kris wasn't a willing participant."

There was silence for a moment. "Are you saying that Anderson turned Kris against his will?"

"I thought you knew?" Ross knew he had just fucked up.

"No, I didn't. That's a crime. It's almost as bad as rape. How could he not bring charges?"

"It was his choice and he made it. Probably because he didn't want to make waves within the vamp community. If there was one thing that Kris hated, it was making a fuss about things."

"He was kind of that way, wasn't he?"

"He's not dead," Ross said sharply.

"Of course not," she replied. "Right now, he's just missing. I'll tell Garner, and he'll get right on it."

"Thank you," Ross replied. "Please let me know when you find something."

"We will," Lily said, and then she ended the call. Ross went over to Kris's recliner and threw himself down in it. It was awfully comfortable. He just wished he wasn't feeling so crappy. Tomorrow he would go to Charles's property and try to find his love. He had to. There was no other choice.

CHAPTER 14

Ross had made it onto Charles's property. He could see the large house across the massive lawn. His dragon's eyes could see far better in the dark than human eyes. It was about one o'clock at night and moonless, so he was glad to have this adaptation. He made his way across the lawn knowing that they wouldn't be keeping him in the house. Ross needed to check the barn and all the outbuildings. The first one was a small shed. He opened the door carefully. A quick examination told him that there was no one in there.

The second was a tool shed. It was also empty. Finally, he came to a large barn and looked inside. There was someone in there. He sniffed the air. It smelled like a vampire was sitting in one of the horse stalls. Ross entered the building and looked into the stall. The figure sat in the dark, watching. He sniffed the air again. That wasn't Kris's scent. The creature rose and drew a sword.

He had no choice. Though it was painful to do quick transformations, he began to change. His body elongating, his legs stretching and bulging claws at the end of the fingers. A tail unfurled from his back end, and his face elongated into a muzzle. It was like torture as things stretched and pulled; like being on the rack. It was both natural and terrible with the pain that it brought. Moments later, he was a thirty-foot dragon, covered in bright orange scales and a black strip of hair going down his back.

"The dragon?" A woman's voice said, "Charles said you might come around."

"Did he?" Ross said in a gravelly voice.

"He also said that I could kill you."

"Where is Kris Kellman?"

"Kellman is dead. We killed him last night."

"Proof?"

"Go to Union Cemetery. We buried what was left of him. Left a Marker there with the name Kris Kellman. He's there, you'll find him. But not if you're dead."

She charged with the sword in hand. He struck out with one of his massive claws. He managed to get it past the sword, and it slashed through her face. She screamed. While she was distracted by the wound, Ross spread his wings and took to the air, crashing through the roof of the barn. He flew back toward the city. He had to know if it were true.

***

He went to the place that the vampire has specified. What he found inside almost made him vomit. Charred remains with a severed head. This would be a way to kill a vampire. Severing the head was always necessary to be sure that the vampire was dead. Charles had murdered Kris, and there was nothing Ross could do about it.

As he stood there over the grave of his lover, he pulled his phone out of his jacket pocket and dialed Lily's number. When she answered, all he could muster was, "Kris is dead." He stood there with the phone to his ear, not speaking, not thinking. Tears leaked from the corners of his eyes.

"Where are you?" He heard Lily ask.

At first, he didn't answer. Finally, he came back to himself enough to say, "in a graveyard, standing over the charred remains of someone I loved." He finally managed to tell her where he was. Then he ended the call. The phone fell from his limp fingers as he stood there in shock. His mind froze and didn't reawaken. An hour later, he came back to himself to find a pretty blond woman standing next to him. "Lily?" He asked.

She nodded. He put his head on her shoulder and wept. The life that he thought he was starting with Kris had already ended. His heart had never been so completely shattered.

CHAPTER 15

There was no escape for Kris. He knew that he wouldn't be left unscathed, or in fact alive. When Charles entered the warehouse with Anna and two other vampires carrying a coffin, he knew that this wasn't going to end well.

"Well, look who decided to show up," Kris was weak, but he could still break out some sarcasm as he slumped back against the metal chair, head hanging. "What the fuck do you want?"

"You know what I want," Charles walked right up to Kris, "I want you to tell me where you hid that information."

"You know it would bring you down."

"The dragon didn't have it. It's interesting that you would set him up like that. Is it even real?"

"I don't know. Were the families that you slaughtered in Aberdeen real?" Kris asked, knowing that it would prove that he knew things that could indeed bring Charles down.

"What do you know about that?" Charles was angry. He grabbed a fist full of Kris's head and forced his head up. "What the fuck do you know about Aberdeen?!"

"All of those women and children that you and your nest killed, just for the thrill. My God. Scotland was in an uproar for years over that. You really shook up the late eighteenth century." Kris smiled at him as best he could. "Are you convinced?"

"Tell me where it is!"

"I can't do that," Kris said, "It pisses you off doesn't it?"

Charles punched him hard across the face. It hadn't broken his jaw, but it certainly hurt far more than it would if he were at full strength. "Ow," he said as he exercised his jaw a bit, "Just going to attack me while I'm down, eh?"

"You're not making this easy on yourself."

"Oh, I'm sorry. Am I supposed to make your kidnapping and torture of people easy?" He shook his head, "go fuck yourself."

"Actually, I vamp-napped you, as I think you pointed out the last time," Charles said, giving one of his smirky handsome smiled. God that vamp was hot.

"You should still go fuck yourself. Then again, knowing you, you probably do all the time and love it." Now he was thinking smutty thoughts about the vampire who had him chained to a chair. *Damn my vivid imagination.*

"Kris," he heard Anna say from behind Charles, "just give him what he wants, for Christ's sake."

"Shut up, you dumb bitch," he didn't like himself for saying that. Not to the woman he had once cared so much for. She had it coming to her, though.

"You're no good for yourself, are you?" She said.

"No, not at all."

"I'm done," Charles said, "Do you have the knots?"

Anna came up beside him and handed him a thick rope with three giant knots in it. Kris couldn't hide his fear this time. "If you stick me in that box with those knots, you will kill me. I won't last one year let alone three thousand."

"Then make a good decision and tell me where the information is."

"I can't do that!"

"Then you must be punished. It's too bad. I don't wish to kill you. I created you so that we could be together, you know. I loved you, but you ran away from me and have since continued to fight me."

"You lie!" Kris cried, "You never loved me. You wanted to control me."

"Maybe I did. But you can't say whether I loved you. Maybe I would have loved to control you. You were beautiful. You still are."

"I am not!" He was surprised that anyone would think him beautiful. He had never considered himself beautiful. He was plain, and he had always known it.

"You think you're not beautiful? That's too bad. You certainly won't be once you've spent several years in a coffin. Take him off the chains," he told his cronies, "it's time to do what we came here to do."

The vampires were both taller and stronger than him as they released him from the chains. He struggled as best he could, but he knew that he couldn't escape them no matter how hard he tried. He kicked and fought as they put him in the box. Then Anna threw in the rope full of knots, and his fight was over. He held the knots tightly in his hands, unable to let go. Anna stood over him, shaking her head. "You should have given him what he wanted."

They set the lid on the coffin and carried it a short way. It was only a short distance from where they had been. The hole must have been pre-dug. All they had to do was lower the coffin in, and the dirt began to pile up on top. Then...complete darkness. He had been buried alive, and with the knots in his hands, there was no escape. His mind panicked, but his body could not. All he could think was, *help me, please, someone? Anyone!!*

CHAPTER 16

Anna was annoyed. She had just buried a former lover. While she and Kris had never had a wonderful relationship, they had loved each other. Or at least she had felt that it was love. Now she felt though that he didn't really feel it was love, or if it was, it wasn't good enough somehow. She resented him for that. Little asshole. Now her asshole brother was trying to implicate her in the murder that she had set him up for. She was sure that while she was working there in his apartment killing the man she had taken that Zeke had been unconscious. Another little asshole. She sat on the sofa in Charles's lounge and dug her fingers into one of the arms. Her nails were nearly ripping into the fabric.

"You're harassing my sofa," she heard Charles come in behind her and turned around to glare at him, "don't look at me that way, dear."

"Zeke is trying to screw me."

"Is that right?" He said, sitting down beside her, "so how did you fuck up, eh?"

"How did I fuck up?" She asked, "You're suggesting that I fucked up?"

"This was your thing," he said, "I told you that you should have just killed him. He's a fucking pain in my arse."

"I couldn't just kill my brother!" She had never felt more like slapping him.

"Why not? I did. It's freeing. In fact, I killed five of my brothers and two of my sisters. Family is baggage that you can always do without."

She did slap him this time, "you asshole."

He just smiled at her, "you massive softy. I feel sorry for you."

She got up and began to walk out. "Don't, I don't need your pity."

"Yes, you do," he called after her. She ignored him. *Asshole...*

***

Anna was angry and worried. She was sure that her brother would do whatever he could to put her away. She knew when she chose to take up with Charles that this might be the case. That he might drag her down into the depths when his crimes finally caught up to him. She was just sorry that she helped him to commit some of those crimes. She couldn't blame him for that. Her actions were her own. In seven hundred years she had learned that blaming others for your own shortcomings got you nowhere.

She felt guilty about what she had done to Kris. She thought several times about going and digging him up. That perhaps he could still be convinced not to destroy Charles and her with whatever information he might have. She knew he wasn't lying about it. Kris would never make something like that up. If he said he had incriminating information, then he had it. Damn...she just wished that she could have gotten the answer out of him rather than having to destroy him in such a barbarous manner. Some part of his soul was still human, she could tell. Taking such a light from a vampire world that was mostly darkness was a tragedy.

She took a walk in the woods on the fringe of Charles's property. It was late summer. The late afternoon sun filtered down through green leaves. Little birds sang in a nearby tree. Out under the full sun, it would have been far too bright for her eyes, but here under the trees, on the little walking trail, it was perfect. She listened to the bird song as she walked along. It was beautiful. Simple. A glimmer of happiness to her. She smiled. Zeke still loved bird song.

Then she remembered that even if Zeke got out of jail, they would probably never be on friendly terms again. She had betrayed him. She had killed someone and made him think that he had done it. She didn't know how he remembered that she was the one who had been there. It was a bungle on her part, and if it ever came to it, she would have to pay for it. She loved Zeke, but he had gotten in the way. Or was that merely what she was made to think? Had Charles manipulated her into believing that she had to get rid of Zeke?

One of the little birds flew from its hiding place in a nearby bush. She grabbed it as it passed by her head. It had a black hood and a white breast and belly. A Junko. The creature struggled in her hand. "I've gotten myself into a bind, little friend. I betrayed my brother, and now it has come back to haunt me."

The bird stared at her through small, black panicked beads of eyes. It continued to kick and struggle. "I suppose I did bring it on myself. I also betrayed and murdered my friend Kris." She petted it on the head, smiling at it in her hand, "do you think that either of them could ever find it in their hearts to forgive me for what I've done?"

She knew she wouldn't be getting an answer, even if she wanted it. She stared down at it for a moment into its little black eyes. Then she let it go. She decided then that if she had to, she would go down fighting, but her days of killing the innocent were over. She would face the consequences for her actions, but her little friend would fly another day. She stood there for a moment under the trees and listened to the bird song again. *I'm sorry, Kris. You were innocent. As innocent as that bird. I can't let you fly away, though. Please forgive me.*

She walked back toward the house, content in her decision to face whatever may come next for her as she should. What was done was done. Now for the difficult part.

***

Charles didn't like to admit when he was worried, or when he was jealous. Right now, he was both. Not only that, but he was jealous of someone who was basically dead. For some reason, even though he was often a gloomy Gus, everyone fell in love with Kris Kellman. Even he had done so once. He was more than willing to admit it. When he had taken Kris off the roadside that night, it had been with the intent of creating a partner that would be with him for all time. Sadly, Kris wouldn't love him and had always seen him as a monster. *The little bastard.*

Charles lay back on his bed. Anna had left the house in a huff. He had to admit that he was the one who had screwed that up. He was flabbergasted that even though Kris was never coming back, she still refused to get over him. He was dead or would be soon. When they had begun this plan by getting rid of Zeke, it had all been so simple. Once Kellman got involved with his "information," things had changed. If only he had stayed out of it. Then again there was no predicting his involvement. He decided to become involved. Charles had thought of just killing Zeke several times but had chosen to leave his fate up to his sister. She had fucked up. This wasn't his fault.

106

The bedroom door creaked open, and Anna laid down on the bed and curled up beside him. He continued the stare up at the black velvet canopy. "You alright?" He asked.

"Yeah," she said, "I think I'll live. At least for now."

"That's good to know."

"Well, a little bird told me that it's time to face up to my own fuck up."

"What little bird?" He was curious as to who she'd been speaking to about this.

"An actual little bird. I took a walk and found a Junko along the trail."

He laughed, "that's lovely."

"He was a better listener than you."

"Somehow I'm not surprised."

She cozied up next to him, "I think we've been putting up with each other for far too long."

"Forty years is not a long time," he said.

"It can be," she replied.

"True, I suppose."

"I love you, Charles, but boy do we ever put the fun in dysfunctional."

"That's what I love about you."

"Thank you, my love."

He held her close, smiling to himself, "you're welcome, my love."

CHAPTER 17

Kris was alone with nothing to do but think for the first time in a very long time. He looked around his box. There was nothing to see and would be nothing to see. Right now, he was worried that he would never see anything ever again. He closed his eyes tightly. He was pained from starvation, being poisoned and that last beating he had. He needed to save his energy. He was glad that he did not need to breathe, but that wouldn't make things any better. He was sure that within a year if he did not go insane, he would probably be dead.

He tried to focus on anything other than the dark. He closed his eyes, thinking that it really didn't matter what kind of darkness he was looking at, it would still be dark. He wanted to move, but he knew he would be unable to do so. He wanted to yell, but he knew that the magic within the knots bound him both in body and voice. If he could just fall asleep, it would be better. It would be better. He squeezed his eyes closed, hoping against hope that he would fall into sleep.

He finally did, but it was by no means peaceful. It was a memory that he had wanted for so long to forget. The night his wife died. They lived outside of the town of Marlborough on what was Kris's father's estate. They were wealthy, happy and had a lovely child. Tonight, they were walking in the summer heat back to their home from a friend's house. It was a lovely evening. Their carriage had broken an axle on the roadside, and they'd been forced to walk. He was dressed in his good suit, and she in her beautiful scarlet dress that he loved so much. He did hope that it wouldn't get too dirty as they walked. Also, Kris knew that there was something that Angela wanted to tell him.

"We should be in the carriage," Angela said, "I should have waited for it to be repaired." She was tired of walking, he could tell. It was fourteen ninety-eight, and everything was a good step away. "I never should have let you talk me into this." She looked over at him and smiled.

He put his arm around her and held her close, "come on then. I'll help you."

"I have news," she said as they walked.

"What news would that be?" He asked her, though he was sure that he knew.

"I think your wish for a son will soon be fulfilled. I am with child again."

"My God,' he hugged her closer, "A son would give me so much joy."

"You are happy then?"

"How could I not be? You are giving me a gift. You are giving us a gift."

"I am glad that you're happy," she said.

Kris had always loved her. Since the day they met. She was sweet and warm and loving. All the things that Kris had always looked for in lovers. Their fathers had arranged the marriage for reasons advantageous to them, but it was a good match for Kris and Angela. They were lucky to love each other. Many couples that they knew certainly didn't. "We should move quickly, my dear

Angela. The sun is going down quickly. It'll be getting cold soon."

They hurried along the road until they met a woman who was running in the opposite direction, screaming loudly. Her white dress was covered in blood. "What in God's name?" Kris watched as she passed. "There must be some kind of attack going on."

"Maybe we should turn back," Angela said, gripping Kris's hand tightly in fear.

More people started to run in their direction, white blurs covered in red, screaming as they went. "Yes, I think that's a good idea," Kris said. He turned to walk in the other direction when a fist slammed into the side of his face, making his teeth clatter together as he flew off into the nearby field. His head bashed into a rock where he fell. He almost passed out when he did, but then he heard his wife's scream. He had to get up; he had to save her! He got to his feet with difficulty his eyes unable to focus at first. Moving made him want to vomit, but he limped back toward the road. When he reached the road, he saw a man in a long dark cloak with a hood bent over his wife. At first, he thought the man was raping her, but she did not struggle, or scream or make any effort to fight. Her voice was gone.

The creature who knelt over her rose. She was covered in blood, eyes staring into nothingness. Kris's wife was dead. And the man who'd killed her had blood still upon his lips. "You have killed her!" Kris cried, "you demon! You've killed my wife!"

The monster smiled at him, it's keen blue eyes boring into him. Kris should have fled from that abomination, but he couldn't. He was stuck, Mesmerized by those eyes. The creature stepped toward him, his fine cloak billowing in the light breeze. He looked to be a nobleman, but the blood on his lips made him a monster. Still, Kris did not run. He backed away a few paces but held his ground. He didn't carry a sword, nor any firearm. He would not run from this thing, though he knew that he should.

"You are brave, for a human," The creature said, "I am Charles. My brethren and I have wreaked much havoc tonight. That was your wife?"

"She was, and I loved her dearly."

"You stand here, ready to die? Unarmed and weak against one of my power."

"God will protect me, demon."

The monster smiled. He then advanced with great speed upon Kris and grabbed him by the throat with one hand, lifting him up. The thing could have killed him. It probably should have killed him. Instead, it looked into his eyes and seemed to be lost for a moment. "Your eyes..." It said, "I have never seen such peace." It loosened its grip but did not let Kris go. "You will be coming with me. I wish to keep you for a while," he said. He then squeezed tighter until consciousness left Kris.

***

When Kris woke up next, he was alone in the dark, lying on a cold floor. His cloak was torn as were the rest of his clothes, and there was blood all over him. He checked his body for wounds. He was bruised and sore, but not wounded. He wondered where all the blood had come from. He tried to get up when he heard the clinking of a chain. That was when he felt the weight of the cold metal around his neck. He was chained to something he couldn't see in the pitch blackness. He followed it the chain, pulling as he went, and nearly tripped when he encountered stairs. Kris made his way carefully up to what he imagined was the top. The chain was attached to a solid piece of furniture. He felt it and determined it must have been some sort of chair. He squinted his eyes and tried to make out anything in the darkness. Even in the very dim light, he could tell that the room he was in was massive.

It came to him that he must be in a throne room of some kind, chained to someone's throne. *Where am I?* He pulled on his tether, desperate to get out of that place. Then something else came to him. The memories of what had happened to his wife and the monster who had attacked them. Kris knew that he had to get out of this place, or this thing would kill him.

He pulled and jerked and wrenched for some time, but in the end, he was unable to get free. He gave up, sitting on the seat of the throne. He knew that he probably shouldn't. He didn't know whose throne it was, or if they would be angry that he was sitting in it. All he knew was that he had been taken, and there was no way out until someone came and set him free. He sat on the throne and wept for the life of his beloved Angela. He had loved her dearly, and now she and their unborn child were gone. As if they never were. He would not be able to bury them. He would not be there to comfort their daughter as the family did. He wanted to die and join his beloved. Hopefully, the bastard would kill him quickly and release him to Heaven where he would meet his lover again in God's paradise.

***

Kris was awakened when he was thrown from the throne he had been sitting in. He fell to the bottom of the stairs. He looked up from his place on the ground. Into the cold, blue eyes of the creature that had taken him. He had looked into those eyes the last time they had met, and he had seen hell. There was light now. The light of torches in the cavernous, empty hall. The walls were stone, and there was no other furniture. There was just the hall, the torches, the throne, and him. He appeared to be a young man; handsome, with a beautiful face and deep blue eyes. He could have been angelic; if there wasn't death in his eyes and on his lips. They were red. Naturally, it would seem. The last time, there was blood upon them.

Kris did not want to look at him. He cowered at the bottom of the stairs.

"Let me make something absolutely clear," The monster glared down on Kris as he sat on his throne, "No one sits here but me."

"What do you want with me?" Kris asked, his voice shaking.

"I want you," the monster said, "I have grown weary and lonely, and I wish for a friend."

"This is how you make friends? By killing their spouses and taking them prisoner?"

"Not all the time, no. Sadly, killing is a necessity. You don't have to worry, though. I didn't bring you here to kill you. I wanted a pet to play with for a while. Mortals make the best pets."

"I am not your damn pet!"

The monster reached down and jerked the chain. Kris was pulled forward, falling onto the stairs. "This would suggest otherwise. I am a leader among my people."

"And what people are those? I don't see a person. I see a monster."

"You would. But I am what I am. So that lovely woman was your wife. You did well, didn't you?"

Kris didn't say anything. He turned away from the creature. He knew if he said the wrong thing that this monster would probably kill him. There was nothing to say.

"I'm going to be having friends over for dinner soon. Please try not to scream in terror. It's best if they don't notice that you're even here."

Kris agreed with that and tried to wiggle back behind the stairs again. He was glad that he did when four more monsters came into the hall. Three men and a woman. They were ushering in five bound people who were as scared as Kris but were probably in more imminent danger.

"You have brought dinner, my friends. Shall we?" Charles said. He leapt from his throne and dug his teeth into the neck of one of the victims. What followed was a bloodbath. Kris almost screamed several times during the onslaught. When it was over, there was blood all over the stone floor. Horror filled him, but he dared not move. He wasn't safe in his place behind the stairs, but it was sheltered from the terrible things that were happening out on that floor.

It didn't matter whether he moved. One of the male monsters still noticed him. The abomination had devilish green eyes that were frenzied with a lust for blood and stringy blond hair. "Oh look, another one."

Green eyes advanced on Kris and grabbed his arm, pulling him close. He was about to bite, his fangs glinting in the light when he was suddenly thrown aside. Green eyes hit the wall on the other side of the room, the sounds of cracking bones filled the room as it crashed to the floor. Charles stood over Kris; his arm extended. "This one is mine and mine alone. None of you will touch him or feed off him. Do we have an understanding?"

The devil with the green eyes fled then, leaving their mess behind. Charles relaxed. "They left quite a mess, didn't they?" He gave a long sigh. "Not to worry, though. I'll clean it up."

Charles cleaned it up. Kris sat at the foot of the stairs and watched in wonder. His speed was amazing, rushing back and forth at speeds Kris could barely imagine. He showed incredible strength as he carried two bodies at a time out of the hall. Then he came back and sat on the throne once again. His white blouse was covered in blood. So were his black boots and trousers, but that wasn't as visible. He sat there, a smug smile on his face. Kris looked up at him sheepishly. "I suppose I should thank you for keeping that monster away from me."

"Come up here to me," Charles said, smiling down at Kris, blood still on his face. "Come on then."

"Are you going to kill me?" Kris asked.

"I just saved you. Why would I kill you? Now come up here to me."

That made sense. Also, Kris really didn't have much of a choice. Charles could easily pull him up by the chain. He decided to get to his feet and walk up the stairs. He stood in front of the creature.

"Come close."

Kris didn't want to.

"I'm not going to hurt you."

Kris leaned in a bit.

"My people are called vampires. We are some of the oldest creatures on this earth. We feed upon mortals. That's you."

"Yes, I noticed."

"I do not want to hear you call us monsters again."

"Alright," Kris said.

"If we are to be friends, then we need to be civil."

"Alright, but why do you want to be friends with me?"

"I don't know how, but I can tell that you're special. Very special. Not creature special, but a special mortal. Even when I smell you, your scent is sweet. Odd that you should be so plain."

"I'm not plain."

"Physically, you're very average. I didn't take you for your beauty."

"I may not be glorious, but at least I'm not a monster." Kris regretted those words the moment they left his lips. It was that night that he realized that you never called a vampire a monster, especially if you're at their mercy.

Charles grabbed him by the shoulders. "You naughty puppy. Now I have to punish you." Charles bore his fangs and bit into Kris's neck. Kris screamed as his captor abused him and took from his blood by force. The attack didn't last as long as Kris felt it had. Charles then threw him to the bottom of the stairs.

"I will amend what I said earlier. I won't hurt you unless you deserve it. I suggest you don't make it necessary again. Especially if we're going to be friends for any length of time."

Kris looked up at Charles from his place on the floor and listened to his words knowing that he was doomed. Charles would eventually kill him if he couldn't escape. He knew that there was no way that he could appease the unpredictable vampire. He just hoped that his death would come quickly and be fast as he held his bleeding wound.

***

Kris opened his eyes inside the coffin. The only way that he knew he was truly awake was the fact that he was still holding the rough, knotted rope. His mind wandered back to the dream he had been having. His wife, his imprisonment. He hadn't thought of them in a very long time. He hated that memory. He wished he could forget it as tears began to leak from the corners of his eyes. He wanted to scream, but there was no voice for him. He cursed his mind again. *Fucking mind. Fucking solitude, fucking coffin, fucking Charles!!!*

CHAPTER 18

Ross hadn't heard from Lily in several months, and yet here she was on the phone with him again. Her voice sounded both tired and elated. He wondered what could be on her mind. He was sitting in Kris's recliner again. He couldn't bring himself to move out of Kris's place. It still felt like home. "Hello," he said as he answered the phone.

"Hello," she said, "how have you been, Ross?"

"Good enough, I suppose. I got this security job at a bank, it's not as fun as what I used to do, but at least I get to be near treasure."

"Treasure is good."

"So, what's on your mind?" He asked, wanting to get on with things.

"I'm calling because of Kris."

"Yeah? Have you found the ones responsible?"

"We haven't, I was wondering if you could."

He was taken aback, "You're wondering if I could?"

"I am wondering if you could find that woman vampire. The one that you encountered in Charles Anderson's barn."

"She's the one who told me where to find the body," he then realized something, "you're not convinced that that's him, are you."

"I was sure then, but then I realized something. Why would she tell us right off where his body is? It's true that there's no way to connect the murder directly to Anderson, but you would think that that would still be something that they wouldn't want to give up right away."

"You're thinking that she told us where to find the body so quickly because they wanted us to stop looking for him."

"That's what I'm thinking. If that's the case, then it's possible that the body isn't his. I mean, vamps know other magical creatures. Witches, sorcerers, demons, fairies and other supernaturals could potentially manipulate bones and other things. I bet if I test DNA in the bone marrow, it won't come back as Kris's."

"You're going to exhume the body?" Ross sighed.

"I have to if I'm going to confirm it."

"It's just...he's lived so long, and he wants to rest," Ross shook his head, "I loved him. I know that I failed him due to the inability to curb my lust. I did love him. I want him to be happy in death because I know sometimes he wasn't in life."

"I know," she said, "but please, just give me a chance to test my theory. If I'm able to, will you hunt her? The vampire?"

"I will," Ross said, though he was pretty sure that she wouldn't find anything new. It was too much to hope for. "If you find anything; call me and, I will hunt her for Kris."

"I know you'll probably have to take time off work to do so. I can pay you."

"Keep your money. I owe Kris this." He'd cheated on Kris. Since the day Kris had found he and Zeke together, Ross had hated himself. He deserved his self-hate. Saving Kris wouldn't make that disappear. Maybe it would help a bit, though. "Find something, and I will do what I can. I'm not the law, though. My methods in dealing with her might not be as ethical as the MLD's methods."

"I don't care. Just bring her back alive."

"I will," he rose from his seat and tossed what was left of his donut in the trash. "I'll be waiting for your call; you still have my number?"

"I do. I'll call you when I find something."

He left to go and ready himself for whatever the hunt. Dragons were excellent hunters, especially when they had good reason to do so.

***

Lily finally called and she had everything he needed to find the vampire who'd taken Kris. He had her scent, and he knew where she would have gone if she had crossed the border into the United States. Oregon was the nearest hub for vampires with one of the largest nests in the Northwest. He found them in Grants Pass, Oregon in an old Victorian house. He knew he would never be able to take them all on. He would have to wait until she left the nest and take her while she was away.

He had watched the house from his pick-up for a while, watching the driveway from a forested area. Ross was a little disappointed that he wouldn't get to kill the vampire. The fire inside him wanted to burn her to a pile of ash. What he needed was information. Maybe he would get a chance to decimate her later, but for now, he couldn't take her life, as much as he wanted to.

When he saw her driving a car away from the house, he followed her. When she reached the outside of the town; waiting at a four-way stop, he came out of nowhere and hit her car at full speed, causing it to flip several times and then catch fire. His own car was burning as well, but it wasn't as hot as the dragon fire within him that wanted to destroy his enemy. So far, she hadn't emerged from the car. He stripped off his clothes and transformed, trying the best he could to ignore the pain of the speedy transformation. His large amber eyes fixed on the crashed, burning vehicle and he growled deep down in his throat, trying to keep his fury down.

He ripped open the car with long, sharp claws and pulled the mangled vampire out of the front seat of the car. His claws dug into her flesh which made her scream in pain.

"Where is Kris Kellman? Does he still live?"

"Fuck you, asshole!" She cried. She screamed when Ross squeezed her, his claws digging in like daggers.

"Answer the fucking question!" Luckily no one had driven by. But he had to hurry. If anyone drove by and saw a dragon digging into a vampire, he would be in an arseload of trouble. He clenched his claws around her. "C'mon, woman. We know the body you led us to wasn't his! Now answer me!"

"I'm not telling you a goddamn thing!"

He slammed her down on the ground; twice. "Answer me."

"Charles had him boxed and knotted!"

Ross was taken aback. That was torture. How could Charles do that to him? "Where?"

"I'm not sure," she said, "I wasn't there. He could still be alive, though."

"Then this is all that you can tell me," He said, "We're going back to Calgary, and you're telling them everything that you told me."

"You can't do that, you asshole!"

"Watch me."

He spread his wings and flapped them. Soon he was in flight with the vampire in hand. Thankfully, the journey would only take six hours, as the dragonflies.

***

Sandra the Vampire told Alexander Garner everything when she was brought in by the dragon. While he was glad to know the truth, he was pretty sure that the dragon had tortured her and that wasn't right. He couldn't prove it, and neither the vampire nor the dragon would tell him that, but he was sure that the confession she had made to him was made under duress. This meant that he would have to change the status of Kris's case to open and as a missing person. He had Charles Anderson brought in to see what had been revealed.

"Mr. Anderson," Garner said, sitting across from the vampire in a grey-walled interrogation room, "You've been implicated in an abduction."

"An abduction?" The vampire asked, a smug look on his face.

"Kris Kellman has been missing for three months."

"Who?"

"Don't pretend like you don't know him. We know your history with him."

"We have a history? You know that we have a history?"

The dragon Ross Harris and the vampire Zeke Yohan seem to think you do. That you're the one that turned him and that the two of you had been butting heads as recently as three months ago. Just before he went missing, in fact."

"That doesn't mean I know where he is."

"The vampire Sandra would beg to differ," Garner said, looking the vampire right in the eye, "she says you know exactly where he is. That you had him boxed and knotted. You do know that that's considered torture and is illegal, right?"

"Sandra? I don't know that I remember who that is."

"You're lying to me," Garner said, leaning in across the table, "I don't like it when people lie to me."

"I may or may not be lying to you, but you can't prove it," Anderson got up, ready to leave, "Sadly, you have nothing. I'm done talking, and you will have to pass all further communication through my lawyer."

"Do you know how guilty "speak to my lawyer," makes you sound?" Garner asked as he rose.

"Does it matter?" He asked. Anderson then went to the door and left. Sadly, he was right, they had nothing. Absolutely nothing. Lily and Captain Harris had been watching from behind the mirror. Garner met them out in the hall.

"You know he's right," Garner said.

"Yes," Harris said, flapping her wings quickly in anger, "We have to find him. We have to find Kris."

"When we were looking into Kris's disappearance the first time, we looked into Anderson's properties."

"What did you find out?" He asked

"He owns a few warehouses out at the ass-end of nowhere. Something tells me that Kris might be buried near one of those."

"We'll have to get warrants."

"And Anderson will fight us all the way," Harris said, "but let's do it."

"I'll get right on that," Garner said. He looked over at Lily, "Send me the information and I'll take care of it if you trust me with it."

CHAPTER 19

Kris knew he was in a dream again. They all seemed to be memories that he wanted to forget. He wondered if it was because of the magic of the knots that he was forced to hold. They did torture him. He could not release them from his hands, which were cramping badly now. He was having to relive every moment of his imprisonment at the foot of Charles's throne. This was going to be bad. He knew exactly how it was going to end.

Charles had provided him with fresh clothes, a little bed, and food that was good enough. In fact, it was pretty good given the fact that pretty much everyone else had just about nothing. Meat, vegetable, just about anything he could want. Wine was always a fine treat. But it didn't change the fact that he was a prisoner to a monster who hurt him and fed off his blood. He knew it was just a matter of time before Charles killed him. Until then, he had no other choice but to play his part in this farcical game.

One night, Charles sat with Kris after he had finished with his meal. Kris knew the vampire would not feed off him right away. He was still wary, though. He watched Charles as he sat on his throne. Kris sat right by its side like he insisted whenever he was in the hall. Kris was sure he had been there at least a few months, but this is the first time that he and the vampire had been alone together in the hall. Usually, there were others. Kris had questions and this might be the only time he would get to ask them.

"You said you are a vampire," Kris said, "what is that?"

"You have seen what we do," Charles replied, glancing down at Kris, "we feed off of mortals, like yourself."

"But what about the sun? Is the rumor true that you will burst into flames if you go outside in the sun?"

"That is a myth. I go out in the sun quite often. Also, you can't kill me with a wooden stake or fend me off with religion. The only way to destroy me is to take my head. There is some magic that can affect us adversely. Dead man's blood is quite harmful, as is knotting. Putting us in a coffin with a rope tied in a string of knots. It takes one thousand years just to undo one. Not feeding is also harmful, but it won't kill us...usually."

"Why are you keeping me?" Kris asked, lifting up the chain that bound him, "why won't you just let me go? Please, you seem to be a good vampire. Let me go."

"No, you are my friend and my blood slave. You cannot go."

"I'm what? A blood slave?" Charles had never said this to him before. The term made him shudder. "You can't do this. I'm not a slave!"

"Maybe not out there," Kris pointed toward the door to the hall, "but in here, you are mine. You are my friend."

"I don't want to be your friend, monster!" Kris cried. He had made a mistake once again. He could see the rage in the monster's eyes.

Charles rose from his throne and hit Kris hard across the face. He fell down the stairs. Charles followed quickly, and when Kris hit the ground, Charles kicked him in the ribs; not hard enough to break them but hard enough to hurt. Charles grabbed a fist full of his hair and pulled him up. "What did I tell you about calling me that?" He asked calmly. Kris was surprised that he was so calm. He was also taller by at least a head, and it was uncomfortable being forced to look up at him.

"I'm sorry," Kris said, "so sorry."

Charles released him, "you're a good boy, but you should really consider not making me so angry."

Kris fell to the ground again, "I'm not a damn dog."

Charles shook his head, "Kris, I have you leashed and collared. Are you sure about that?"

Charles left Kris lying on the ground and gasping. When he had recovered a bit, he went and sat on the lowest step. Kris couldn't help but weep. He'd never wanted death more in his life. He wanted to be free, but he knew that would never happen. He realized that sulking would do no good and wiped his eyes and went to his little bed. This was hell, but as long as he lived there was still hope. Rescue wasn't likely because there probably wasn't anyone looking for him and it wasn't likely that someone would just find this place by chance. Kris had to tell himself that it was possible because he wasn't ready to die yet, even though he told himself that he was.

***

He was awakened because someone was gripping his wrists painfully. He was being pulled from his bed by an unknown assailant. He opened his eyes and saw the blond vampire that he had encountered the first night he was there. The creature was forcing him to the ground. What was this? He was for Charles only! "You can't!" Kris cried, "I am for Charles alone!"

"Are you?" Green Eyes asked, "I really don't care," he said, "now you are mine." The vampire bore fangs and plunged them into Kris's neck. He screamed, but he was not strong enough to push escape the ravenous beast. He was determined to kill Kris, and there was nothing Kris could do to keep his life from fading away as his strength left him and his vision began to blur. Then someone grabbed Kris's would-be murderer from behind and tossed him aside. It was Charles, and he went after the other vampire and did not hesitate to rip off the other creature's head.

None of this mattered to Kris, though. His neck had been badly gashed, and any hope of stopping the inevitable was gone. Charles rushed to his side, but there was no hope, and soon, Kris's eyes closed. Some part of him hoped forever.

***

Kris tasted blood. He was sure that it was probably his own given his recent injury, but it wasn't. It was from a wrist shoved against his mouth. The blood came from a gash in it, and he was willingly drinking from it. What was this? He pushed it away. "No!"

"I saved you," Charles said, looking down on him, "now you can live."

"I don't want to live! Kill me! I don't want to live! I don't want to live like this!"

"Eternal life is now yours. A little gratitude would be nice."

"For what? You have turned me into a monster!" Kris pulled against his chain savagely. It broke. He ran from that place even though Charles called after him to stop. Kris was now free. Or was he? He was now an unholy abomination, a loathsome creature. He hoped that someone would kill him soon. He truly did not want to live this life of sin.

***

Kris opened his eyes in the darkness of his coffin gripping the knots hard in his hands, tears leaking from his eyes. He hadn't cried this much in a long time. He was also growing weaker. He was starving, wounded and was running low on any hope that he would see the dragon he loved ever again. He wanted to see the sun again and smell the air and the flowers and the water. He didn't have to breathe it, but he liked a nice breeze. He cursed himself, and the magic that he knew held him in this place. If he could just let go of the knots, he could probably find some way to free himself from the coffin. *Fucking knots...*

Kris was crying again. Whatever this magic was, it was far more powerful than he was. He wanted to die. He wanted someone to come and end him. This torture was far too terrible and being forced to go on like this was just too awful to contemplate. He hated himself; he hated Charles, and he hated everything. He tried to move again. His stomach was churning with hunger. He knew that he would not join his wife and children, even in death, but at least it would be over. *Come back, come back and kill me you cowardly assholes!!!*

His mind drifted to Ross. He would never see him again. Was this suffering worth holding out for that chance that someone might find him? All he knew was that right now nothing was worth it and he just wanted everything to be over. Everything... *Fucking life!*

CHAPTER 20

Lily sat in the passenger's seat of Ross's car. She noticed that he hadn't gotten another pick-up. The small sedan didn't seem to fit him very well. He was a larger man, tall and burly, so seeing him in a little car was a bit odd. He had officially started working for the MLD as a general law enforcement officer. Lily had asked him to drive her out to one of the buildings that she wanted to go search. It had been tough, but they had acquired the warrants that they needed, and now they were headed over to an old warehouse that was well off the beaten track. Alexander was searching another place on the far side of the city. It was just she and Ross. It was winter now, and the roadside was covered in snow.

"I'm afraid," she said, "of what we might find, if we do find him."

"You're worried that he's dead, aren't you?" Ross didn't look over at her, but she could tell from the sound of his voice that he was pained by the very thought that Kris might be dead.

"Kris has already been dead once. I don't know if I could bear it if he were to die again."

"You really care about him, don't you?" The dragon asked, "I love him too. I should have loved him better. But I couldn't control my lust. I betrayed him. Some part of me will never forgive myself for that, but I'm glad that we were able to be lovers and trust each other..."

"Don't say in the end," she interrupted him, "it may not be over yet."

"It's been six months, and who knows what condition he was in when they put him in. I know that I should be hopeful. I can't help but be realistic, though."

They pulled up to the building. It was late in the day. The warehouse itself was nearly falling over. The glass that had once made up the windows was now shattered. The forest around it was overgrown and dark. The branches were barren, and the ground was covered in a dusting of snow. Lily was sure this was the place. *It would be an excellent place to hide bodies.*

She got out of the car, and Ross was soon by her side, his nostrils flaring as he tried to detect anything that smelled like vampires in the air. He walked toward the building, and continued to search the air for scents, Lily was close behind him as he pulled open the door. The darkness inside was almost complete, but Ross could smell vampires. In the middle of the room was a chair with chains lying around it. Ross sniffed it and his eyes widened in recognition as he caught Kris's scent. "Kris was here! He was in this chair!"

"What?" Lily said. She couldn't believe what he was saying. "He was here?"

"I can smell his blood. We must look around more. He might still be here."

They kept looking, going into the next room. The ground dipped and caved under their feet; their shoes sinking into it no matter where they stepped. Ross stood over one of the sinking areas and his nostrils flared widely as he tried to catch as much scent as he could. "He's here!" Ross said, "and he's not the only one. All these places where the ground is sinking, people have been buried. I don't know if they're human people or vampires, but they're down there."

She looked over at him and then around the room. "This room is huge. There could be several people buried here."

"Yes, there could. Which is why we have to hurry."

"I'll make a call and get some help," she said.

"I'll start digging," Ross cried.

Lily took her phone out of her pocket and called for back-up. They had found him. She was just worried that when they dug him up, he would be dead again.

***

Kris had been dreaming again. For the first time, he had met Ross. In the nineteen forties, he had recently broken up with Zeke. The vampire that he had known and loved so much had cheated on him with another. He had left the home that they had shared for many long years and now wandered the streets of London as he had once done long ago as a feral vampire. Now he was just lonely. He sat down on a park bench and stared off into nothingness. They had been together monogamously for nearly a hundred years. How could Zeke betray him like this?

So, he sat there, and he stared into nothingness, pondering why someone he had loved and trusted would betray him...again. He'd experienced the same thing with Zeke's sister who'd cheated on him as well. He let out a deep sigh. Luckily, the only one there to hear it was him. It was five o'clock in the morning on what looked like a lovely spring day. He was sure if there were people around, he would be getting looks from people. Staring into nothingness wasn't chic in any time period in any place.

He barely noticed when a tall, brawny man with glasses sat down next to him. He really didn't want to until the stranger spoke.

"Something troubling you?"

At first, Kris didn't know if he should answer the stranger. He looked over at him, a large man in a dark suit with a pleasant enough face. Or at least the smile on it was friendly. "There's no end to trouble in my life. It seems to follow me wherever I go."

"My goodness, that does sound maddening," the stranger said, "I've had my fair share of troubles, mate. All you can do is carry on."

"That's true. And I have had to carry on from a great many things. Most recently, my lover."

"He a vampire too?"

"What?" Kris was taken aback. He gave the man a hard look, "who are you and what do you want?"

"Me? I just want to have a conversation. But if you must know, I'm a dragon."

"A dragon?" Kris asked in disbelief. "I've never met a dragon before."

"I've encountered a few of your kind before," the dragon said, "my name's Ross. Who might you be?"

"My name is Kris," Kris said.

"Well, it's good to meet you, Kris. Nothing better than a chance meeting with a friendly face."

"Even if that face is filled with sorrow?"

"Those are some of the best," Ross said, "when faces can still be woeful, you know there's still a bit of humanity in them. I would say soul, but dragons don't have souls."

"Neither do vampires."

"Imagine that," Ross said with a smile, "I imagine you and I could be friends, Kris."

"I reckon so," Kris said. *I could probably use a friend right now.* As the two spent time together, they became far more than friends, and then the betrayal. *Why? Why can't any of you just love me? Stay with me? Be mine? Am I really so terrible?*

He heard something and knew that it was time to wake again. If he could.

***

Ross found that he could dig far faster in dragon form. All of these quick transformations were wearing on him, but he had to do this. He stripped off his clothes, and in a matter of moments, he was in his dragon form. His large clawed feet were sinking deeper into the ground as he stood there. Ross started to dig wildly, dirt flying around him in dark clumps. Finally, his nails scratched wood that he knew must be the lid of a coffin. His next transformation was back into a human as he finished digging the box out of the ground. With his dragon strength, he pulled the coffin out of the ground. Lily walked back into the room, her eyes widening with hope as she saw Ross standing over the wooden box.

"Are you staring at my ass?"

"Put some clothes on," she said, "back-up will be here soon."

He quickly did as she asked. She ripped the lid off the box as he did so. She was stronger than she looked. There was Kris, his eyes closed, his hands holding a rope with three knots. He was covered in blood and looked painfully thin. "Kris!" She cried as she knelt down by the side of the box. He didn't appear to be moving at all. Ross reached down and tried to pick him up, but he wouldn't come out of the box.

"The knots." Ross said to Lily, "take the knots out of his hands."

Lily reached for the knots and tried to pull them away, but she couldn't. Ross realized that she wouldn't be strong enough, given the strength of the magic. He let go of Kris and grabbed the rope instead. "I'll pull the knots away; you pull him out of the box, okay?"

"Okay," Lily said.

Ross reached in and grabbed the knots. He yanked them hard, and he flew back across the warehouse as they were finally released from the vampire's grip. That was powerful magic. He rose and noticed that Lily was pulling Kris out if the box. She sat and cradled his head in her lap. He still wasn't moving. "He's not breathing," she said, patting his face with her hand. "Wake up, please."

"I don't know whether he needs to breathe. Somehow, I don't think so. But he's not waking up either."

"Breathe Kris," she said, "or at least show me some sign that you're alive." She stroked his face with her hands. "Please, wake up for me."

Ross watched, trying to figure out what he could do to help his friend, but there was nothing to do. They had to wait. Finally, Kris stirred in her arms. "Kris?" Ross asked.

"Am I dead?" the vampire mumbled.

"Not yet," Lily whispered to him, "you're still here." She had a smile on her face. Then Ross realized something. If Kris were awake, he would probably be starving.

"You need to get away from him," Ross said to her.

"But he's just woken up," Lily said.

"Yes, and he'll be starving. You're human."

His point was clearly made when Kris lunged at her, fangs out. Ross was just able to throw himself between them. He held Kris tightly. "Go get the chains from the chair."

"You want to chain him?" She asked, astounded.

"If I don't, he won't stop until you're dead. Now, do as I say!"

Lily went and got the chains; Ross wrapped them around Kris and locked them tight. He then carried the thrashing vampire out to his car. The moment they stepped out into the dim sunlight, Kris screamed, squeezing his eyes closed. He continued to whimper in the light.

"Light isn't supposed to hurt vampires," Lily said.

"He hasn't seen any for six months," Ross said, "they're far more sensitive to it." He carried Kris to the car and shut the vampire in the trunk. "He'll be safe there for now."

"I'm so sorry, Kris," she said, setting her hand on the trunk lid.

"He'll understand," Ross said. Back-up arrived a few minutes later. Ross handed Kris over the MLD knowing that they would take care of him. For now, Ross had to do what he could for the others, hoping that there were others there that would be as lucky as Kris. No one deserved to die like this, regardless of whether they're monstrous.

CHAPTER 21

Zeke was still in prison. They were refusing to let him go under the guise of it being for his own protection. That pissed him off to no end, but there was nothing he could really do about it. He asked for canvas and paint so that he could work on something he liked while he was locked away. They allowed him that, and he immediately put brush to canvas. It didn't matter what he tried to create. Somehow, the picture morphed into Kris. Whether he was a figure in the painting, or it was a portrait of his face, it was him. Every canvas, every time. He stared at the last one.

"Goddammit, Kris, I can't get you out of my head!" He threw it against the wall in his cell. The wooden braces supporting the canvas broke, and the picture tore. He felt guilty and got up off the bed where he had been sitting. He walked over to the fallen canvas and looked into the eyes he had painted again. They were Kris, through and through. Zeke had always been able to catch his essence on pictures. He figured that was why Kris hated them so much. They proved that he wasn't a monster. That there was still a soul somewhere in him.

Now he would never see those hazel eyes again. He stared into them. "I'm sorry," he said, looking at the now ripped and mangled canvas, "I fucked up so many times, I hurt you deeply, and for that, I may never forgive myself. I don't expect you to ever have forgiven me. I just wish that I could see you one more time. So that I could tell you that I'm sorry."

He dropped the canvas on the floor again and threw himself down on the bed, frustrated.

***

Zeke woke to the sound of someone opening his cell door. It was Dent the fairy; he was alone this time, but he looked like he had good news of some kind. Zeke got up from the bed. Dent had a big smile and reached out a hand for Zeke to shake. "I have good news for you."

"Hello to you too, what good news have you got?"

"The MLD has found the location of several vampires that have been boxed and knotted."

The color drained from Zeke's face. Tortured and possibly dead vampires were good news? "What?"

"That's not the good news...well, it is, and it isn't. The point is, they found your friend Kris Kellman. He's alive, or at least he was when they found him. He's on his way to the magical hospital now."

"My God," Zeke wasn't sure how to react. It was as if he had asked for a miracle and it had been granted, "this is a miracle."

"That it is," Dent said, "and it means your ordeal may soon be over. Charles Anderson is already in hot water for having committed this crime. He and your sister have fled as far as I know. Once we get the files that Kellman has been keeping, it should be enough to warrant execution for Anderson at least. As for your sister, I couldn't say, but that means you'll no longer be in need of protection. You'll be free as a bird."

"I can't believe it..." Zeke was in shock. He stood there, staring at the floor in disbelief.

"Believe it," Dent said, "It's almost over." The fairy left him then. Once alone, Zeke did the only thing he thought a sane person could do. He fell to his knees and wept. Kris was alive!

CHAPTER 22

Kris needed to open his eyes. He didn't want to. Wherever he was now, the lights were extremely bright which was just another type of torture. Open them he must. He could feel warmth again and he felt "full" for the first time in months. That was a nice change from starving to death in the dark. His eyes were blurry, but he could tell that he was in a sunlit room. The walls were white. He hated white walls. They just reflected the light which was already too bright. This was a hospital room in the magical hospital where they took all supernatural creatures. There was a needle sticking into the vein in the crook of his arm as bright red blood flowing through the clear tube attached to it. He'd survived, but he was hardly ready to get up and rejoin the world. It would probably be a while before he was back to his old self.

The door creaked open, and he heard the light clacking of heels as someone came in.. He didn't open his eyes as the visitor sat in the chair beside his bed. He finally opened his eyes and his eyes wandering over to see who sat in the chair. "Lily," he said with a smile, "It's good to see you."

"Kris, you're awake."

"Yeah, I'm awake. Where's Ross?"

"I'm so happy to see you awake. Ross stepped out for a bit to get you some things. He'll be back soon, I'm sure."

"I'm just happy to hear your voice," he said, "I never thought I would hear it again. I was not sure that I would hear anyone's voice ever again."

"I know. I knew somehow that you were alive. We never gave up on the chance that you might be."

"I'm happy about that. God, it's so fucking cold."

"You've been in the ground for several months. Summer has passed. It's winter now."

"I don't like winter," he said wearily, "vampires never feel the warmth, but we always feel the cold. I just want it to be over."

"Well, we have a few months left, Kris."

"Have you arrested Charles? Surely you have enough evidence to charge him."

"We do," Lily said, reaching over and caressing his face, "we have him on several counts of murdering his own kind."

"His own kind?" Kris asked, "but I'm alive. Who did he kill?"

"Kris, you weren't the only one who was buried there. There were fifty others buried there as well, along with a few humans. Half of the vampires died."

"Dammit..." Kris said, "I thought I was the only one he had done this to."

"Apparently he had far more enemies than you thought."

Kris didn't want to think about that. Then he noticed the ring on her finger. "That's lovely," he said.

"Kris, Alexander and I got engaged while you were gone. I'm..."

"Congratulations," he said. He didn't want her to say she was sorry. She hadn't done anything wrong. "I'm happy for you."

"Thank you, Kris," she said, relieved. "You look tired. I think I should go. Leave you to rest."

"It was good to see you," he said. Then she was left him to think. He hated being alone with his thoughts. A while later, the doctors came in and informed him that the next three months or so of his life would be spent in this bed. Kris felt helpless.

A little bit later, Ross came in. Kris didn't want to see anyone, but he wasn't about to tell Ross to go. "Hello Ross," he mumbled.

"You sound annoyed."

"I'm just tired, my love. Also, I'm going to be stuck in this fucking bed for the next three months!" He wanted to throw something or break something. Ross handed him a paper bag. "A present?"

"Open it."

Kris did, and he found a wedge of dark chocolate in there. "You know me too well," he said with a smile.

"That's because you never change, Kris."

"I don't?"

"No, you don't."

"You haven't really either."

"Wonderful. Well, I'm glad that you're okay."

"No," Kris said as tears began to fall down his cheeks, "I'm not okay. I never thought I would see you or anyone else again. I never thought I would see the sun or feel the breeze again. So many times, I wanted to die. I had to relive so many things that I wanted to forget. I wanted to die, but I couldn't."

Ross came over and hugged Kris in his bed. "I'm so sorry. God, you have no idea how sorry I am. About everything. I wanted so much for you to be okay."

"I'm alright," Kris said, "I just...I was just..."

"I love you, Kris. I will always love you. I think you already know that, but I wanted to say it out loud. A tiny piece of a human soul that still lives within you. That's why you can taste things and feel the warmth and how you can care so deeply."

"Then why does everyone leave me?"

"I don't know," Ross said, "no one is perfect, Kris. Everyone has their reasons. I'm just glad that you're still here."

"So am I," Kris said, "and I'm sort of surprised."

"Well, hopefully, Charles isn't going to get away with it this time."

"Didn't they arrest him?" Kris asked.

"We were going to, but he's made a run for it. He's probably in America now. He might even be in Europe by now."

"He escaped?"

"It's just a matter of finding him, Kris. We'll do it. In the meantime, they're releasing Zeke Yonah."

"What about his sister, Anna?" Kris asked.

"Anna Yonah? She seems to have disappeared with Charles."

"I see," Kris said. "all we have to do now is retrieve the actual files. I'm more than ready to bring a few people down with that information."

"Wait, the files are real?" Ross asked him.

"Of course, they are! Do you think I'd actually make something like that up?" He shook his head, annoyed. "The files are real. I just need to get them."

"Where are they?"

"You want to risk your life again?" Kris laughed.

"If you can assure me that they're real, then, I will go and retrieve them for you, and I will take reinforcements."

"They are real. I doubt that you have to worry about Charles again, but take your reinforcements back to the bank, it's there, it's just in a different box. Then take it directly to the Captain."

"It's at the same bank that you already sent me to?"

"Yup."

"Do you have any idea how annoying you are?"

"I have a pretty good idea, yeah."

"Are you sure that you want me to take it to the Captain right away?"

"I think so. It's best that it all comes out. None of us are saints."

"Then I'll go, and I'll be back," Ross said. He left Kris then. Kris knew that once the MLD got that information, nothing would ever be the same again. He would probably be seen as a traitor, but it was time for the truth to come out. He laid back in his bed, alone with his thoughts once more.

CHAPTER 23

Zeke was finally released from MLD custody. The first thing he did was go to the hospital to see Kris. He had been set free because of the information in Kris's files. Arrests were being made, and as long as Zeke promised to help in some of the investigations, he was told that he would not be prosecuted. The morning he was freed, he went back to his home for a shower and a change of clothes. He had been able to shower in MLD jail, but he didn't like the fact that he had to be naked in front of other people when he did. At least at home, he could take a nice long shower and put on fresh clothes. They didn't make him wear the traditional orange jumpsuit, but he was really tired of the three outfits he was allowed.

He was sure that Kris wouldn't give a damn if he were just wearing jeans and a tee-shirt. It was winter. No one was looking under people's thick jackets this time of year. The MLD had done a great job of cleaning up his apartment. There wasn't a speck of blood to be found in there. They had even gotten it off his paintings. It was amazing! Despite the fact that bad things had happened in this apartment, it was still home. Also, he was pretty sure that if he did want to sell it, he would get that security deposit back after all.

After showering and dressing in a plain blue tee-shirt and putting on his brown padded jacket, he headed out to the hospital. When he got to Kris's room and went in, Kris was asleep. His face was so very beautiful, and peaceful, regardless of all the tubes he seemed to be hooked up to. Zeke sat down in the chair for a moment and just watched as Kris slept. After a while, he got out of his jacket pocket a little sketch pad that he always carried with him and began to draw. Kris had the perfect face for this kind of picture. He slept so beautifully.

For some time, Zeke just sat there in peace, drawing Kris. Finally, Kris stirred and opened his eyes. Zeke watched his face for a moment as he woke. Kris smiled when he saw Zeke sitting there. "Hello, old friend."

"Hello Kris," Zeke smiled back, "I'm happy to see you."

"God, I'm so happy to see you too. You have no idea,"

"I was so worried that I'd never see you again. And that I'd never get to say..."

"You'd never get to say what?" Kris had his concerned face on, Zeke knew that he had to continue.

"I was afraid that I'd never get a chance to say I'm sorry. For everything." tears began to fall, "for this, for cheating on you, for stealing your dragon, everything."

"Zeke, it's alright."

"No," he said, "it's not alright."

"Oh, for fuck's sake, Zeke. I don't really want to get into this right now."

Zeke was taken aback, "I was just..."

"It's okay, Zeke," Kris said a little more softly, "I'm just glad to be alive right now."

"It's a miracle," he said.

"It's Lily not giving up is what it is."

"She made this happen?"

"She and Ross."

"Ross's been in on this?" Zeke didn't even know that Ross was involved.

"Yeah, he's the one who dug me up."

"Well, thank goodness for that." He would have to find Ross and thank him.

"I'm kind of thinking that maybe Ross and I might try something again. I know that we didn't end things off very well the last time, but I'm just hoping that..."

"That what? Things have changed? If you feel like it's the right move, you should go for it."

"I think I will. Zeke, you know I love you and I always will."

Zeke cocked his eyebrow in surprise, "Yeah, I love you too and always will. It almost killed me when I thought you were dead. Don't do that to me again, please."

"Oh, I'll do my best. I'm just a little pissed that Charles and Anna wussed out and ran off."

"I know. I could go try and track her down," Zeke suggested. He knew he would never find them, but he could at least make the offer.

"I don't think so Zeke," Kris said, "It'd be too dangerous. What have you been sketching?"

Zeke showed him the paper, "It's you."

"Good lord," Kris smiled looking at the paper, "yeah it is. I think that's the best one you've done."

"You're a good subject," he said, "I always do good ones of you."

He felt it was about time to let his friend rest again, so he got up, "well, I'm so happy to see you alive and well, Kris, but I'd better be off."

"Thanks for coming to see me," Kris said.

"I'll be back in a couple of days," Zeke said, "for now, sleep well."

CHAPTER 24

Kris laid in his bed. As an immortal, he wasn't used to being incapacitated or hooked up to machines meant to restore his health. That was a human thing, not a vampire thing. And as he watched the blood being fed directly into him, he shook his head. Dead man's blood had done this to him, and the damage was incredibly slow to reverse given that he was exposed to it for so long. *Fucking poison...*

There was a knock at the door. "Come in," he said, not even concerned with who it was. He was so over visitors. He didn't want to remember that he was an invalid who had been rejected by the woman that he had once tried to kiss.

The door opened and a young woman walked into the room. Or at least she looked like she might have been human. She was lovely, with long dark hair and dark, endless, eyes, but she didn't smell human. She announced herself at the door. "Kristof Kellman, my name is Lydia Danse, I'm from the Magical Investigative Services in the United States."

"Are you? You smell like a feren. You must be a feren. You keep your wings well shielded, but I can still smell you. What brings you to my bedside, Ms. Danse?"

"You're right," she said as she dropped the shielding spell on her wings a little. They were large and burgundy, like a great red moth's wings. "I am a feren."

"They're beautiful," he smiled up at her, "you should take them out more often."

She giggled, "I wish I could, but this is not a world where we can just walk around with our wings out. Speaking of things that are out there now, your friend, Ross Harris brought in files that he said had been compiled by you a couple of days ago and shared them with the MLD. The MLD, in turn, shared them with the MIS and other magical law enforcement communities around the world."

"He found what I sent him to find? How does that bring an American agent to my hospital be here in Calgary?"

"When we were going through the information sent to us, we came across a name associated with a human trafficking case we've been working on."

"Human trafficking case? I think I found a reference to it myself in my research. I just didn't know why he was doing it. They say younger blood is sweeter." Kris said, confused. "Come and sit if you would like," he indicated the chair at his bedside. She gratefully came and sat beside him.

"Yes, actually more like a kidnapping ring. Children have been disappearing. Children from good families. They're being taken by vampires."

"For what purpose?" Kris shook his head; this didn't make any sense. "For food?"

"For progeny."

His eyes widened in shock. "What the fuck? Vampires don't do that. We don't create child vampires. They're unable to survive on their own. Adult vampires have it hard enough. I didn't want to think he could be that vile. If he were using them for food, that's vile enough, but as children for vamps? It's just not right. Now that I know for sure…"

"The name that we found in your files that linked up with the case was Charles Anderson. I know he's on the run, but I understand that you two had a history. I was wondering if there were anything else you might be able to tell me?"

Kris shrugged, "I followed his movements for a very long time, but I have become lax in my attention in the last few years. I am not as familiar with his more recent associations and doings. But I can't believe that he would involve himself in something like this."

"I know, it's unbelievable, but it is happening. I'll be sticking around Calgary for a while, see if he mysteriously re-appears. I'm hoping he'll show up so that we can question him on his contacts in the United States," she got up from her chair and offered him her hand, "It's been a pleasure meeting you, Mr. Kellman."

"It's been lovely meeting you as well," he said, shaking her hand. Then she left him.

The afternoon sun was filtering through the blinds in Kris's room. He was incapacitated, and now, there was another mystery wearing on his mind. The snow that had fallen a few days ago was now melting. The sun reflecting off the white surface wasn't as bad as it had been. He still felt trapped, though. He hadn't been this lonely and distraught since his wandering year in London when he had been a feral. That was when Anna and Zeke had found him and saved him from himself. God, he missed the days when things were simpler, and he was just a vampire, not a vampire with responsibilities who may have brought about the downfall of some large figure in the vampire hierarchy. *Fucking hierarchy…*

It was almost night when someone else knocked on the door. It had been a long day of disturbing news and fairy nurses who were annoyed that they had to waste their healing talents on a vampire. *Annoying bitches...* "What?" He literally yelled at the door, expecting more abuse.

"Well hello to you too," Ross said as he poked his head in through the door.

"Ross," Kris said, embarrassed that he had snapped, "sorry about that, come on in."

"Are you sure?" He asked, "you don't seem to be in a very good mood."

"I'm fine," Kris rolled his eyes, "just frustrated. Come in."

Ross came in and sat in the chair next to Kris's bed. He had a brown paper bag in his hand. "What's that?" Kris asked.

"I brought you something," Ross reached in and pulled out a large candy bar. He handed it to Kris. It was a huge dark chocolate Hershey Bar. Kris opened it and broke off a section, putting it into his mouth. He savored it. A single tear fell down his cheek.

"My God, thank you for this. It's been a couple of days. You spoil me so badly." He let it melt slowly, finally, he said, "I hear you found the files."

"There was one in there on me," Ross said, "I thought for a moment about taking it out, but I decided it was best for everything in there to come out. There were so many terrible things in there. Rape, murder, the non-consensual turning of vampires, massacres, those criminals deserve what they get."

"I'm proud of you," Kris said, "You're a good dragon. And you killed livestock. You didn't rape and murder virgins, or burn entire towns to the ground, or anything like that. Speaking of which, a woman from the MIS in the United States came to see me today. She was here looking into Charles's association with a child kidnapping ring. They're kidnapping children and turning them."

"What?" Ross said, a look of disbelief on his face. "Why would anyone do that?"

"Apparently, vamps want kids now."

"That's ridiculous. They can't just turn kids. That's disgusting!"

"Yes, it is. If I ever see Charles again, I'm going to beat him with a stick until he tells me what his involvement is with all of this."

"I don't know that we'll ever be seeing him again, though. He's murdered several people, including many of his own. You weren't the only one we found down there, remember?"

"I don't want to," Kris said, shaking his head.

"Several other arrests have been made. Other high-ranking vamps on charges ranging from murder to non-consensual turning of people. You've done well Kris."

"Have I? Or have I betrayed my own?"

"Don't be like that, Kris. If anything, they betrayed their own. You're just making it right."

Kris gave him a smile, "you're right. I just worry...about everything."

"I know you do," Ross said, "and that's part of the problem. You focus too much on the bad to stop and refill your heart with joy." He reached over and took Kris's hand, "I know I fucked up, but it almost killed me when I thought you were dead. I love you. I didn't know if I would be able to live without you. I cried, Kris. I fucking cried. In front of that woman, Lily."

"I..." Kris was not sure what to say. Should he say what he was truly thinking? If he did, it meant that he was opening himself up to be hurt again. Was the risk worth it? "I love you too."

Ross looked into Kris's eyes. Kris patted the bed beside him. "Get in," he said, "I want to be close to someone."

"Are you sure? I won't disturb anything?"

"Oh, I'm sure not. And if you do, we can always get a bitchy fairy to come in and fix it. Now, are you going to join me?"

"Sure," Ross got up from his chair and took off his tattered old jacket, leaving it on the chair, He laid down on the bed next to Kris who immediately burrowed into him. Dragons were always warm, and Kris had always been able to feel Ross's warmth.

"My God, you're so warm," he said, burrowing closer into the dragon. "I have missed you more than you know."

"You just like me because I literally light your fire."

Kris chuckled, "yeah kind of. Do we know what we're doing?"

"We're starting out again for the third time. You were dead. And it created such a hole in my heart that I couldn't even bring myself to move out of your place. I love you. And I think I've decided that it would be best if we marry. I may not be able to claim you, but at least I can be bound to you through marriage."

Kris looked up into his eyes, "Wow, I wasn't expecting a proposal. I certainly wasn't expecting it here and now. I must ask you though. Are you sure? Can you bind yourself to me? Be mine forever, or at least as long as you shall live?"

"I will make you that promise now. I will be yours forever and ever. Until death takes me."

"And never shall we part again?"

"Never again."

Kris tilted his head up and kissed Ross. Together again. It probably wasn't the wisest decision he could have made at this moment, but he was going to do it. He had lived when he shouldn't have. He had stared death in the face once again and had come out the other side. Now he was ready to begin his life, not just with his lover, but with his husband.

CHAPTER 25

A month later, Ross took Kris home. He had been at Kris's place the night before to prepare things for Kris's arrival home from the magic hospital. He did dishes, washed clothing and the bedding, and re-arranged some of the furniture. The next day, he carried Kris into the apartment as if they had just been married, which annoyed Kris to no end. As they entered the living room, Kris squirmed in his arms, "you didn't have to carry me, you idiot."

"I know I didn't have to. I wanted to," Ross gave him a smile and set him down on his feet. "Happy to be home?"

"You moved my stuff..."

"Yeah, I brought some of my things over. Like my TV and stuff. Nothing really that big."

Kris looked at the TV that he had installed, "I don't like it, it's a massive monstrosity."

Ross rolled his eyes, "oh for goodness sake."

"I don't remember asking you to install this."

"Well, if we're going to live together, I need something more than your charming personality to entertain me."

"Are we having a fight already?"

"This is not a fight," Ross said, "It's just a little tiff. You'll get used to it."

"What? The tiff or the massive monstrosity that you've put on my wall?"

"Both," Ross said, walking over and throwing himself down into the recliner. "You're not exactly a master decorator. I mean you have a white sofa. You're a vampire for fuck's sake! Why on earth would you have white furniture? And a Laz-y-Boy, eh? I fucking love it, but it doesn't actually fit in with anything you had in here. I mean, will you please decide on whether or not you're a posh prat or a lazy bum, because I can't tell."

Kris gave a loud laugh. He covered his mouth with his hand, continuing to giggle behind it for a moment. Ross chuckled and motioned for Kris to come over. Kris walked over and took his hand, sitting on the dragon's lap. "Well, at least I can still make you laugh," Ross said, and then he stole a kiss. Kris relaxed back against him. It was going to be alright, he decided. Ross held him close, his warm arms felt good around Kris, who cuddled down into them. "I love you," he said, and he took the dragon's lips in a kiss again.

The dragon gathered him into his arms again and carried him into the bedroom again. He kicked the door closed as they entered and took Kris, gently placing him on the bed. "The doctors don't think I am able to make love again just yet," Kris said, though he could feel his growing erection superseding any doctor's recommendation.

"That's unfortunate," The dragon sat down beside him on the bed and began to kiss him again.

"Yeah, I suppose," Kris said between kisses. "Eh, screw doctors. C'mon, my love. Let's have some fun."

CHAPTER 26

"He betrayed me," Charles said as he paced back and forth nervously, "they know about everything, even the vamp kids."

Anna sat on the four-poster bed nearby. They were staying at a friend's place outside of Montreal. They had only just escaped Calgary before the magic police had shown up, and now they were on the run. This place was small compared to the mansion they had left outside of Calgary. It was a roof, though. The room was dark, and Charles's bare feet made a slapping sound on the hardwood floors as he walked back and forth. He was bothering her, he could tell from the look on her face. "Don't give me that fucking look."

"You should have known that all of this would eventually catch up with you, Charles. And I'm going down with you."

"Needless to say, if I ever meet that little scrotum sucker again, I will fucking kill him."

"You can't. Kris is fucking a dragon now. That thing will rip your head off. Why didn't you kill him four months ago, when you had the chance?"

He came to a full stop right in from of her, "because I love him and I wanted to believe that he could love me too."

"You love him? What the fuck?"

"Yes, I love him. The moment I looked into his eyes five hundred years ago, I fell in love with him. That is why I chose him as my blood slave and companion. I wanted him to learn to love me. So that when I did turn him into one of us, we could have been companions forever. Some part of me still hoped for that. I was going to give him six months and then dig him up...I..."

"You sad, fucking, softy!"

"Please, don't start," he said, sitting down beside her and putting his head in his hands. "I fucked up, alright?"

"Then maybe we should think about making it right."

"And how do you propose we do that?"

"We kill him. It's too late to save ourselves. With the evidence they now have against us, it's prison regardless. We can at least take him down with us."

"You want to kill Kris?"

"It would be the right thing to do."

"How do we get our hands on him?"

"We take his little girlfriend. The coroner from the MLD. It will be perfect, and then we can destroy both before we go."

"You really want to take that chance?" Charles asked, "We could be captured or killed if we go back."

"We will eventually be captured or killed anyway. This way, we can at least destroy the one who destroyed us."

"You are a devious creature, aren't you?" Charles said as he leaned over and kissed her.

"Very much so," she said between kisses. They would take him out, and then, come what may, at least they would have achieved that.

***

Zeke had never expected to hear from her again. Both of them knew that she had fucked up far too badly for him to ever forgive her. When he got the call from Anna, he was surprised. He was at home, rehanging the pictures that he had to take down when he had fled so many months ago. The phone was sitting on a nearby chest and vibrated loudly when the call came in. He was just finishing up adjusting the picture. He reached over and grabbed the phone, not even checking to see who It was. "Hello," he said, still looking at his handy work and trying to decide if the picture was straight on the wall.

"Hello Zeke," he heard her voice say.

He froze, "Anna?"

"Yeah, Zeke, it's me."

"What do you want, Anna?" He wandered over to a nearby armchair and sat down.

"Oh, nothing really. I just wanted to say that I was sorry. For everything, really. I fucked up, didn't I?"

"So, you're just sorry that you fucked up trying to get me killed? Not the fact that you were trying to get me killed."

"Don't be so dramatic, Zeke," she sounded exasperated, "I wasn't trying to kill you. I was trying to come up with some plan in order for you to be out of the way, but alive."

"By setting me up for murder?"

"Yes, Charles kept telling me that I shouldn't bother. That I should just kill you. I told him I couldn't. That you're my brother and I just...couldn't."

"This is fucking ridiculous."

"Is it? I'm sorry."

"And stop apologizing!" He wanted to throw the phone he was so angry, "what the fuck do you want? And I mean, what do you really want?"

"I guess what I really want to say is goodbye. We won't be seeing each other again, and we're obviously not going to be making up."

He shook his head, "you bitch. Goodbye, and I hope to God we never see each other again. You're my sister, and I did love you, but you fucked me over, and no, I will not forgive you. Now fuck off!" He hung up the phone. Good lord, she was ridiculous sometimes. He picked up the phone again and called Tim Dent. When the lawyer answered the phone, he sounded a bit flustered, "Dent here."

"Hey Tim, it's Zeke Yonah. I just got a weird call from my sister, Anna. Should I report it to the MLD? I mean, it's probably not important, but..."

"Call Alexander Garner at the MLD and report it. He'll definitely want to hear about it. I would do it, but I'm swamped right now."

"So, you think I should?"

"Yes, I think you should."

"Okay, thanks. I'll talk to you later then."

"Goodbye."

Zeke ended the call. Fucking Anna. She always made everything so difficult.

***

She hadn't expected him to forgive her. It would have been foolish of her to expect such a thing. He was right, she was a dumb bitch. She was also fully ready to go down in flames for it. Now she and Charles would return, and they would destroy Kris Kellman for everything he had done. Of course, all he had done was to expose them. Still, he had no right to do that. His death wouldn't change anything, but it would make her feel better for a while.

CHAPTER 26

Ross laid on the sofa, Kris was close by his side, resting his head on Ross's chest. Ross squeezed him. Kris was close to being his old self again. Since they had begun their relationship anew, things had been going well. Ross knew that Kris didn't really like TV but had taken to watching it with him anyway. He kind of liked watching *Into the Badlands* now. They were draped in a blue fleece blanket, and Ross could tell that his love was close to sleep.

"You alright?" He asked, "you want to go to bed?"

"No," Kris said blearily. He yawned.

"You would probably be more comfortable if you went and laid down."

"I don't want to lie down," Kris said, "I want to be here with you."

"Alright," Ross said, kissing the top of his head. He left Kris where he was. Soon he heard his love breathing heavily in sleep, "silly man. Don't worry, I'll take care of you."

The next day, they found time to be together. Kris laid back on the bed, Ross was deep inside him. Ross was kissing him deeply on the lips and had a firm grip on Kris's wrists on either side of his head. He was on the edge of a slow, beautiful bliss. It wasn't the fast, feverish sex of a young couple. It was the slow tender love of a mature couple, and it was so close to helping Kris to his release. He closed his eyes and relaxed, as he continued to kiss his love. His phone vibrated on the nightstand. He moaned, more out of annoyance than pleasure.

"You want to get that?" Ross said between kisses.

He moaned his disapproval, "mmm-mmmm..."

"It could be important," Ross said again.

"No..."

Ross stopped moving, "Kris, we really should..."

Kris wrapped his legs around Ross's waist, pulled his hands out of Ross's grip and put a finger to his mouth to shush him. "I said no. I am not getting out of this bed until you make me come. Now make me come or stay here forever."

"How do you know I don't want that?" Ross smiled against his finger.

Kris smiled back at him. "C'mon then," he said, "let's get this show on the road."

The phone had stopped vibrating sometime during their renewed lovemaking. Twenty minutes later, they were well into a cuddle session; Kris was on the brink of sleep. The phone started to vibrate again. Kris didn't open his eyes, but he felt Ross reach over him to get the phone. "Hello," he said. Kris listened. "What? Who took her? What the fuck?" A pause, "you want us to come in?" Another pause, "They're friends, I'm sure Kris will want to be in on this." Another pause, "alright, give us a bit and we'll be right in." He ended the call.

Kris opened his eyes, "who was that?"

"That was Alexander Garner. Someone grabbed Lily off the street. She's gone."

"What?" Kris said.

"She was taken. Alexander wants us to come in. Get up and get dressed," he slapped Kris's ass cheek playfully, "and put some clothes on. No one gets to see your nude splendor but me."

"Asshole..." Kris rolled out of bed with a smile. He needed a shower but didn't feel he had time for it. He threw on some clothes and was soon ready to go. As they rode in Ross's care to the MLD, Kris fidgeted, "We should have picked up the phone when it first rang."

"What?" Ross asked.

"The phone. I refused to let you get it. What if it were her?"

"I checked. It was Garner."

"We still should have gotten it."

"I doubt it would have made a difference, Kris."

Kris shook his head, "God I hope you're right."

When they finally arrived at the MLD, Kris used his vampire's speed and dashed like a blur into the building, and up the stairs into the Captain's office. "Captain, what's going on? Have you found her?"

The feren nearly jumped out of her skin when the vampire suddenly appeared next to her and Garner as they stared at a board that had all the evidence posted on it. "Dear Lord, Kris," she said, grabbing her chest, "you scared the hell out of me!"

"Sorry, Captain. What do we know?"

"It's good to have you back," she said, "you're still supposed to be on medical leave, but if you're up to it, we'll be glad for the help.

"Charles Anderson is back," Garner said, "he took her. He called me and told me as much."

"What does he want?" Kris asked.

"He wants you, Kellman," the dragon said, glaring over at Kris.

"What?"

"He wants you. He said he would trade her if we delivered you. He even said he would surrender to us."

"You don't believe him, do you?"

"He kidnapped my fiancé..."

"I know..."

"He gave us a delivery place."

"Then hand me over," Kris said.

"What?" Ross asked as he came through the door, having finally made it up to the Captain's office, "hand you over to who?"

"Charles..."

"Kris, we can't just hand you over to Anderson," the Captain said.

"Thank you." Ross looked relieved.

"But you can use me as bait," Kris said, "you can use me to find her and to get him."

"I assume you have a plan," Garner looked unimpressed.

"I do," Kris said, "but you'll all have to trust me. Especially you, Ross. Can you do that for me?"

"Do I have a choice?" He looked pissed. They would have to have a conversation about this.

"No, I'm sorry."

"Then, we have no choice," Ross said. He walked out of the room, a hurt look on his face.

"I have to go after him," Kris said to the others, "just give me a moment, and I'll be back."

"Okay," the Captain said, "but you need to hurry. The time Anderson set up for the trade is tonight. We have to strategize."

"I know. Just one moment." Kris went after Ross. He found him standing outside the front door, leaning on the crumbling white molding of the door, smoking a cigarette. "You smoke?"

Ross gave him a sharp look, "yeah I smoke, especially when I'm stressed."

"I'm sorry."

"You're sorry?" Ross flicked his cigarette, knocking the ash off the end of it, "You just handed your life over to a mad vampire. A life that I thought you knew means quite a lot to me. He will kill you this time."

"I have a plan," Kris said.

"Sure, you do," Ross didn't look convinced as he dropped the cigarette and stepped on it. "I hate those fucking things."

"Then why do you smoke them?"

"Because I can. I mean, for Christ's sake; I'm a fucking dragon. What, am I going to get cancer and die from it?"

"I don't think that's how it works."

"Of course, that's not how it fucking works! Now come on. Let's get your plan started. I sure hope you know what you're doing."

"Yeah," Kris said, following Ross back into the building, "I hope so too."

CHAPTER 27

Lily was really, uncomfortable. She had woken up in a strange house in what seemed to be a dining room chair with her hands bound behind her and her ankles tied to the chair legs. She sat in the middle of a large ballroom with wood floors, dark, heavy curtains, and a large crystal chandelier hanging directly over her head. It might have been beautiful, had she not been a prisoner. She was pretty sure that she knew who had taken her. It was confirmed when Charles Anderson walked into the room.

"What do you want, Mr. Anderson?" She cried, struggling in the chair.

"Don't do that; you'll hurt yourself..."

"Answer the fucking question."

He gave her a surprised look, "alright. I suppose I owe you that."

"You "suppose?"

"Yes, so I will tell you," He sat down in front of her with his legs folded in front of him.

She glared at him, annoyed. "This is about Kris isn't it?"

"I want him. I want him to come here after you, and when he does, I will kill him, and then I will surrender. I'm not going to harm you any more than I already have."

"You're going to surrender?"

"I have to," he shrugged, "I don't want to spend the rest of my life running. And seeing as I will live for a very long time, I really don't want to spend the rest of eternity running."

"But you're going to kill Kris. Why?"

"Because I want him. I have always wanted him. That is why I chose him five hundred years ago to be my blood slave and my companion. I wanted to spend eternity with him," he said. "I didn't mean for things to happen the way they did. I would have turned him eventually, but I wanted it to be his choice."

"Then why are you killing him?"

"Because he will never love me as I love him. He set me up to be killed, so I am going to kill him."

"You don't have to do this," she said, "no one has to die. Please, just let me go and disappear. I promise you I will make sure that you have a decent head start."

"That's a wonderful offer," Charles laid back on the floor. "Sadly though, I don't think you can help him this time." He didn't look up at her but continued to speak. "Vampires don't usually retain any part of their human souls. Kris has retained some of his soul. That's what makes him so special among our kind. He can be...human where the rest of us can't. It's too bad that I have to end him but end him I must."

"No, you don't. Please, don't do this. Don't throw your life away. Do you really want to spend eternity in prison?"

"Prison?" He laughed, "no, my dear. I will be put to death. The only thing that a vampire with my kind of crimes would get."

"No, no. I know that they wouldn't do that."

"Of course, they would, my dear. I am sorry that I had to get you involved with this. Know that I do respect you and what you do, but it was necessary. I had to get his attention. Now that I have, he will come, and he will die. Apologies for that as well. I know you like him. I still love him too. But there are some things that can't be forgiven." He jumped up from his place on the ground. He patted her on the head like she was a friendly dog, "thank you for your understanding, dear. Now I'm going to call your boyfriend and tell him that I have you. Be a good girl and cooperate with me as I set things in motion."

She rolled her eyes as he took her phone. She gave him Alexander's number, and he called. She was so pissed that she cried when he put the phone up to her face. She knew that she shouldn't be. It would just worry Alexander, and she didn't want to do that. Then the call was over, and the vampire ended the call.

"Thank you," he said, "for your cooperation. This will be over before you know it."

"This can be over now," she struggled again, but it was no use.

"I know, but I've made up my mind. Just settle in. And just so you know, even if you scream your head off, there's no one around to hear you. My mansion is out in the woods. The dragon Ross found it once, but other than that, it's pretty much out at the ass-end of nowhere."

"Just go away..." Lily said, glaring at him.

"My thanks again, madam," he said, and then he was gone. She tried struggling again, but this vampire tied killer knots.

***

"We shouldn't be doing this to her," Charles said, sitting down on the bed next to Anna who was drinking blood from a wine glass, "are there still blood bags in the refrigerator?"

"There is if you want some."

"I'll go down in a bit and get some," he said, "she's innocent."

"All of our victims are innocent," Anna said, putting her head on his shoulder, "or at least they don't feel they deserve to die like that."

Charles laid back on the bed, staring up at the red velvet canopy, "do they deserve to die like that?"

"It depends," she tossed the glass against the nearby wood-paneled wall and lay back next to him, "some of them do, some of them don't. And no, I'm not going to pick that up. If we're going to die tonight, what the fuck does it matter? Just a bit of broken glass."

He rolled his eyes, "are the others ready? You and I know that this is ending in nothing less than a raid on the mansion. I'm ready to die. I think I've been ready for a while. I just want to know that they are."

"They're your most loyal followers. If they weren't ready to die, they wouldn't be here."

"And what about you?" He reached over and took her hand, squeezing it, "there's still time. You can go if you'd like."

"I'm not leaving you. I've lived for over seven hundred years. Maybe today is a good day to die."

"Then we'll die together. I suppose I should be thankful for that."

"Yes, you should," she said, sitting up,

"I know I should," he continued to lie there.

"Tonight is going to be ugly. Be sure that you're ready."

"I'm ready," he gave a long sigh, "so very ready..."

CHAPTER 28

Kris sat in the back seat of Ross's car, Ross and Garner sat in the front. Kris could tell from the way that Garner was gripping the arms that he didn't very much like the way that Ross was driving. "Could you please slow down," he finally said after the dragon had blown through a few stop signs.

"You want to get there, don't you?"

"Yes," Garner said, annoyed, "I'd like to get there alive."

"Whatever," Ross slowed down a little bit and began to watch the roads more carefully.

"By the way, I called you both several times a couple of hours ago. What on earth were you doing that you couldn't pick up the phone?"

"We were making love," Kris said, rolling his eyes.

"Kris, don't tell him that," Ross chuckled.

"You were having sex in the middle of the day?"

"Yes, we were," Kris said.

"That's far too much information."

"Well, you're the one who asked," Kris rolled his eyes in mock annoyance.

"So, what is the plan?" Ross asked Kris, "you do have one, don't you?"

"Oh yes, we go in there, take down everyone who gets in our way, save Lily, and we don't leave until Charles is dead."

"Wow," Garner said, "somehow I was expecting something far more sophisticated."

"Most of the time, simplest is best," Kris said, "It'll be fine, you'll see."

"I'm just baffled because it's not so much of a plan. It's more like a plan someone would come up with if they didn't know how to create a strategy."

"Oh, I'm sorry," Kris was annoyed again, "is your plan somehow better?"

"I wouldn't say that, no."

"Can we just go with, 'go in and kill everyone'?"

"Fine..."

"God, you're such a ridiculous dipshit."

"No more than you."

"You're both nimrods," Ross said calmly, "now shut the fuck up; I'm trying to drive."

"Whatever," Garner lapsed into silence, and Kris did the same.

When they arrived at the outskirts of the mansion, Ross pulled the car into a wooded area. It was late afternoon. It would be dark soon so they would have to hurry. A cool spring breeze wafted through the trees "It's best if we approach on foot," he said, "far easier to transform in a field than it is a car. And I just got this fucking car, so I don't want to mess it up just yet."

"Understandable," Garner said, "should we transform now?"

"No, not yet. We transform when it's necessary," Ross told him.

"But isn't it stressful to a dragon to do sudden transformations?"

Ross gave Garner a hard look, "you have transformed before, haven't you?"

"Not in a very long time," Garner had an embarrassed look on his face, "I don't like the feel of it, and I don't like heights."

"A dragon that doesn't like heights?" Ross looked like he might smack Garner, "for fuck's sake. You're an embarrassment." Ross walked away, shaking his head. Garner followed.

Kris was hooking a sword onto his belt. He also had a gun in his holster, but the firearm would be useless. Kris would never use their own tactic against them. He would never use bullets doused in dead man's blood to hurt his brethren. He would shoot them though, and that could at least slow them down. He hadn't used his sword in a long while, but back in his earliest days as a vampire, he had become a master swordsman. He just hoped those skills hadn't slipped. He headed off after the two dragons.

He caught up to them just as they were approaching the barn where Ross had encountered the vampire assassin. Kris could tell from the stance that the dragons had taken standing on the lawn that they could sense the vampires, if not smell them directly. They began stripping off their clothing. Kris drew his sword as the transformations began. A moment later a twenty-foot-long blue ice breathing dragon stood on one side of him while Ross's massive orange dragon stood on the other side.

The vampires began to pour out of the barn and arranged themselves out on the lawn in front of the three invaders. One of them, a tall, skinny blond vampire, stepped forward. "Welcome, Kristopher Kellman. I see you brought friends. I am Garreth. Charles has asked me to welcome you."

"You have been with Charles a long time," Kris said, remembering the blond vampire who had attacked him and ended his first life, "the one that Charles killed for attempting to kill me was your brother, wasn't he?"

"His name was Gerard, and yes, he was my brother. He shouldn't have tried to take what wasn't his."

"And now, I stand face to face with you, I will give you a choice. You and all of your friends here," Kris stepped forward a little way past his dragon escort. "I will offer you this one chance to walk away from this place," he said, his hand firmly on the hilt of his sword. "I will give you this one chance to decide if you really want to give up your lives in support of that monster who would kill several of his own kind, and who would traffic children to make vampires of them." The vampires looked at each other nervously, as if considering what Kris was saying and whether they truly did want to go down with Charles's sinking ship.

Garreth spoke again, "here's the thing, Kellman. Many of us are complicit in his crimes. I didn't know about the children, but I sure as hell know about the murders. I helped him bury some of those poor assholes. Sadly, I was away the day they buried you, but I'll gladly bury you after you die in agony this time."

"None of you will walk away?" Kris asked, beginning to unsheathe his sword.

"It's too late for us, dear Kristof. I'll see you in hell." The vampire charged him, his sword flashing in the late afternoon sun. It clashed sharply on Kris's now drawn sword. The other vampires charged the two dragons. Vicious claws swept through the air and blood flew through the air. Heads began to tumble as well. Kris wasted no time in quickly outmaneuvering Garreth, and his head soon joined the others on the ground. He cut down vampire after vampire. He didn't know how many were there, but he was glad that he had Ross and Garner by his side. He never could have taken them all on by himself. When the fighting finally subsided, the two dragons were covered in dark vampire blood, and pieces of at least one hundred vampires lay at their feet. Kris was also drenched in the blood of his brethren but thought nothing of it as he looked to his dragons and whether or not they were ready to move on.

"We need to transform," Ross growled, "we can't do anything in the house like this." He began his transformation and was in the form of a man once again. He was also shaking and breathing hard. The fast transformations were wearing on his strength. He went over to where he had left his clothes and dressed.

Kris went over to him and put a hand on his shoulder, "you should rest."

"I don't need to rest," the dragon said.

"Yes, you do. Just take a moment."

"I don't need a fucking moment," Ross pushed his hand away, "I'm fine." The dragon stalked toward the house, a large knife now in his hand.

Garner came up beside Kris, "are you alright?"

"Yes, but he's not. He's running on adrenaline, and it won't get him as far as he wants it to."

"We'll need to keep an eye on him then."

"Are you alright?"

"I'll live," the dragon said, but Kris could tell that the transformation was wearing on him as well.

"He should have waited."

"There's no time for that now," Garner started toward the house, "let's go before he gets himself killed."

Ross was already fighting inside the foyer of the house, his knife slick with the blood of vampires, several heads at his feet. Kris had his sword at the ready, and Garner had a short sword in his hand. The three of them fought their way in. They were soon right outside the ballroom doors, dead vampires all around them. Kris was right at the door, but he hesitated for a moment. "Lily's in there. I can smell her," he said.

"Then let's get on with it!" Garner cried.

"Anna's in there too. And she's not going to let us have Lily without a fight."

"Oh, for fuck's sake," Ross said, "go in there and deal with it."

"I'll have to kill Anna."

"So what? She betrayed you and helped that jackhole bury you alive. Don't tell me you still have feelings for her."

Kris gave him a sideways glare. He hadn't thought about how he would react in this situation, should he face it. Now he realized that he did still have feelings for her. "You're right," he put his hand on the door handle and began to push it down, "I'm going in there, and I'm closing the door. Do not open it until I say it's over."

Ross watched as Kris walled through the door and closed it behind him. Kris held his sword before him as he carefully approached the hostile vampire who would kill his friend if he were not careful. Anna's blade was close against Lily's throat. She looked calm for one who might soon be facing death. When she finally looked into his eyes, Kris saw something he didn't expect. A look of regret and sadness. "I knew you would come," she said, "that you couldn't resist."

"I'm sorry it's had to come to this," Kris held his sword at the ready, "but you've given me no choice. Give Lily to me, and I may yet let you go."

She smiled at him, "I don't need your fucking pity, Kris. I intend to die here because my time has come. You've seen to that. You've destroyed Charles and me, and for what? The love of fucking humans?" She laughed maniacally, "what a fucking joke. If they knew what you were, they'd destroy you in a second, because that's what humans do. They destroy."

"So have you."

"Have I? I did nothing more than come around to Charles's point of view and supported him in his mission."

"His mission to destroy."

"Get off your high horse and see the reality. We can't hide forever, and once we're out there, wouldn't it be far better if we're at the top of the food chain?"

"You sound insane."

"I was insane enough to love you. Soft, tender, beautiful you. What a fool I was."

Kris pointed his sword at her, "let the girl go. Your quarrel is with me, not her."

Anna took her blade away from Lily's throat. "Come then and fight me."

She lunged at him. Kris blocked the blow but was thrown back against the wood-paneled wall. She was on him in a moment, and he was barely able to withstand her onslaught. He managed to get to his feet, blocking the blows of Anna's sword as they rained down upon him. Then finally, he parried an errant blow and used the opening to cut her hand from her arm. She screamed as both hand and sword went flying. Lily watched in horror as Kris stood over the wounded vampire, sword raised.

Anna was crying, but he knew he had to do it, "I did love you. So very much. I'm sorry for your pain, but this ends now."

"Then do it, you asshole! Stop assaulting my ears with your endless yammering and..." he cut her off by detaching her head from her shoulders. Kris ran to Lily and began to untie her from the chair.

"Lily, are you alright? Did they hurt you?"

"I'm alright, Kris. Are you?"

He looked sadly over at the severed head of his former lover, "I'll live," he helped her up and walked with her over to the ballroom doors. "Garner is out there. He'll take you to the car. We'll get out of here as soon as I've taken care of Charles." He opened the door and found Garner there waiting. Lily ran to him, hugging and kissing him, but Ross was nowhere to be seen. "Where is Ross?"

"He heard something upstairs and went to go investigate. He told me to stay behind and wait for you here."

"Damn," Kris said, "get Lily out of here. I must go take care of Charles, one and for all. Ross went up the stairs, didn't he? Toward the roof?"

"Yes, he did."

"I'll go after him then. I may still need your help. Just get Lily to safety for now."

"Right," Garner took Lily's hand and led her toward the front door of the mansion. Kris saw the stairs nearby and started on his way up. This house was vast, at least four stories. He went to the top where he had to pick a direction. There would be another staircase. It was either to the right or the left. *Left*, he told himself. When he reached the end of the hall, he found it, the stairs going up. On the third floor, they were on the other side. He finally found the door that would open onto the roof. He drew his sword and threw the door open.

He stepped out onto the roof. It was dark outside, but the roof was well lit by thousands of flickering candles. Charles was so overly dramatic. The vanity and self-importance was just pathetic and sad. And in the light of the candles, he saw Charles standing there in a dark shirt and trousers, wearing a long black cloak. At his feet, Kris saw what appeared to be a body. "Ross?"

"I seem to have slain one of your dragons," Charles held his sword over his head, "blessed swords will do that to a dragon. They'll do even worse to a vampire."

"You dick!"

"That's right, Kris. Come get me." Charles charged him. He rained blows down upon Kris, not letting up. Charles's blade slashed his shoulder, the blessed blade creating a burning wound on Kris's shoulder. He'd never felt anything that was that terrible. It was like being stabbed with a firebrand and an icicle at the same time. The dead man's blood wasn't even that bad. He held his shoulder, whimpering miserably. He kept his sword in a tenuous grip as he held the wound. Charles leered down at him, "you see. A blessed blade will hurt you like no other. That may not have been your sword arm, but I don't see you lasting much longer."

Kris held his sword at the ready. It wasn't going to be over until one of them was dead. He tried to get to his feet. "Kill me," Kris said, "why aren't you killing me?"

"I could, but I am enjoying your suffering at the moment."

"You've always enjoyed it. You have always enjoyed my pain. Probably far more than anyone else's."

"You still have a part of your human soul left, Kris. That means that, even as a vampire, your suffering is far more beautiful. Oh, how I would love to taste you again to see if you are still as sweet as you once were."

Kris rolled his eyes, "just kill me, you freakish asshat."

Charles kicked Kris in the chest. He fell to the ground again. "You will die when I wish for you to die. Somehow I am disappointed by your weakness."

Kris got up. It took all his efforts and made him want to hurl, but he did it. He raised his blade. "Come get me, you pathetic piece of shit." Charles charged him again. He was so confident of his win that he did not expect Kris to be able to block effectively. Kris managed it somehow, blocking blow after blow, and finally, he parried a stroke that was aimed at his head, and brought up his own sword, putting it through Charles's. The vampire fell, but Kris still took a moment to detach his head completely from his shoulders.

He then stumbled over to Ross's side. Tears were flowing down his cheeks. He just knew that his love was dead. He held him close, weeping bitterly for his loss. Then he heard it. Ross was breathing. The wound was bad and still bleeding, but the dragon was still breathing. "Alive? Don't you dare fucking die on me, Ross."

Someone tapped Kris on the shoulder. He looked up, expecting to see an enemy, but looked up into the face of Garner. "Kris is he...?"

"He's alive! We have to get him down to the car, but I'm not strong enough to carry him," Kris said.

"I'll get him down there," Garner bent and picked Ross up, "God he's heavy."

"Yeah, he is, we have to go," Kris said. Garner carries Ross off the rooftop, but Kris lingered for a second. He looked down at Charles's head and wondered if he ever could have been what Charles wanted. It didn't matter, though. He was dead, and Kris had to take care of his dragon. Charles was now part of his past that he would never have to wonder at again. *Fucking asshole...*

CHAPTER 29

Ross opened his eyes. He was in a hospital room, and sitting by his bedside was his love, Kris. Kris was asleep, his head resting on his hand as he snored quietly. Ross smiled. He reached his hand out to Kris and realized that he was still in quite a bit of pain. He gasped loudly, which woke Kris from his sleep. Kris smiled and jumped up from his chair when he saw that Ross was awake. He even began to cry; which Ross thought was a little bit overkill.

"God, I thought I had lost you," Kris said, "they said that you might never wake up again."

"Is that what they said?" Ross laughed but was too pained by his wound to do so for any length of time.

"I was so worried that you would be taken from me," Kris bent over Ross and kissed him on the lips, "I'm so happy that you're awake."

"You already said that."

"I know. I'm just so happy."

"That's ridiculous, now sit down before you piss yourself like a happy puppy."

"Sorry," Kris sat again. Then he told Ross about his final encounter with Charles.

"I'm proud of you, Kris," he said, "you took down the bad guy."

"I know. I'm kind of proud of me too."

"It's over then," Ross was happy. His love was happy. Now it was over, and they could go on with their lives with the assurance that Charles would never darken their door again.

CHAPTER 30

Zeke had decided that he would not take Anna back to England to bury her. They had left their lives, family and connections behind a long time ago. If things had been different, he would have taken her home and buried her next to her husband and their parents. Sadly, she hadn't been given a chance at a normal life. They were young when they were both turned against their will. She had been twenty, old for a woman seeking a husband at that time, and he had been twenty-five. They had been turned by the man who would have been Anna's husband. They didn't know what he was at the time. He had chosen her to be his eternal bride, and Zeke had gotten caught in the way of his rampage as the vampire had slaughtered their family.

She had killed him. Zeke knew that she had done it to save him. He wanted to kill Zeke, and he knew it. He had no idea why the vampire had spared him in the first place. He was pretty sure that it was to keep Anna under control, but it hadn't worked that way. She killed him at the first opportunity, and when he was dead, Zeke helped Anna to pick up the pieces of her shattered soul. Kris was the closest thing to a true love that Anna had ever had. It was just too bad that he was too good for her, a point well proven when she tried to torture Kris to death.

Today, as he stood in the cemetery, over the grave of his sister, he was truly sad for her. She had died lonely, and with so many regrets about the choices she'd made. He wept for her as the rain began to fall, "I'm sorry."

"What are you sorry for?" He heard Kris's voice behind him and turned to look at him. He was dressed in a black three-piece suit and was holding a black umbrella over his head, "It's not your fault."

"I was her brother, I should have done better. I should have protected her from herself," he said as he wiped the tears away, "we've always looked out for her."

"You can't control what she did to herself," Kris covered Zeke's head with the umbrella as well, "she made her own choices and walked her own path. She was over seven hundred years old. What exactly did you think you were going to do to dissuade her?"

"You're right," Zeke sniffled, "I'm being foolish."

"No," Kris said, putting his arm around his friend, "You were her brother. You cared about her."

"Did you once," Zeke said.

Kris nodded, "once. In fact, always. I fell in love with her the day I saw her, I loved her when we were together, and it nearly killed me when she betrayed me. I just feel that deeply."

Zeke chuckled, "yeah, I know you do. That's what I love about you."

"I know. You messed up, buddy. Now you can't have this."

"I know. You were far too good for both of us."

"And Ross."

"But you're back with Ross."

"What can I say? Dragons are sexy."

They both laughed at this, "yes they are."

"What are you going to do now?"

Zeke thought about it for a moment. He had thought that he would just carry on as he had before all of this, but then he realized that he hadn't really been doing anything. He had been working as a bartender part-time and selling art the rest of the time just for the purpose of doing so. He didn't need to, he just did it. Also, his world had changed since vampires and creatures he had known for many long years were now being arrested due to the information that Kris had gathered. All of his friends were disappearing. Maybe it was time for something different, "I think I'm going back to England for a while. My family calls. It would be nice to visit the family home and the cemetery. I should tell them about her."

"Tell who, Zeke? They're all dead?"

"That doesn't matter. I can still talk to them. Mother and father will be happy that she has come back to them."

"Do vampires go to heaven?" Kris asked.

Zeke thought about it for a moment, "I don't know. I'd like to think they do. At least I'd like to think she's found peace."

"Of that, I have no doubt."

"What about you? Are you going back to the MLD soon?"

"Yes, I think so. Both of us I think."

"Well, that's it then," Zeke said, "I'll be seeing you again someday, Anna. Until then, take care, sister."

Zeke left her then, with Kris by his side. He was glad that there was somewhere there with him. He didn't know if he could have faced this alone. He still had friends. That was good to know.

***

When Kris got home, he walked in and went straight to his recliner and collapsed. He hadn't thought that Anna's funeral would be so emotional. Charles's certainly hadn't been. Actually, he didn't really get a funeral. They put his body in a crate and shipped it off to somewhere in Eastern Europe. Kris supposed that was where he must have originally been from. He didn't really care. Still, he found it interesting that they would just ship him off like he was a package from Amazon. He kicked off his shoes. He wondered why anyone would want that package. They would probably return it. Getting dead vampires in the mail was probably like getting a box full of vomit.

He kicked back in the chair. People were ridiculous sometimes. It was then that he realized that he could probably do with some refreshment. He really didn't want to get up? now. Why in God's name hadn't he gotten himself a beer or something before he had sat down He laid his arm over his face.

There was an insistent tapping on his foot, and he pulled his arm away from his face. He saw Ross standing at the foot of his chair. He had a bottle in his hand.

"Beer, sir?"

Kris sat up and took the bottle from Ross, "Thanks for this."

"You look nice," Ross said, walking over and sitting on the sofa, his own bottle in hand. "Broke out the three-piece, did you? I think you overdressed just to go and stand there in the rain with Zeke."

"I felt I owed it to him," Kris sipped his beer, "we've known each other for a very long time."

"Yes, I know."

"Did you know I once proposed to her?"

Ross was taken aback, "you did?"

"Yes, I did. I was stupid. I thought we loved each other. I realize now that I just really didn't want to let her go. So, I did a stupid thing."

"It wasn't stupid," Ross said, "It was human. You did the human thing. The emotional thing, the thing that proves that you still have a soul."

"I still have a soul? You think so?"

"Yes, I think so."

"Vampires don't have souls."

"No," Ross said, "dragons don't have souls. We're born without them. Actually, we're hatched without them."

"Hatched?"

"Dragons come from eggs. They're technically more beast than human. It takes a great amount of physical strength to keep us in our human forms and from destroying lesser creatures like mindless monsters."

"You're holding back your ferociousness, are you?" Kris laughed.

"Actually, yes, I am."

Kris couldn't help himself. He let out a long barrage of laughing. "Good for you, love."

"Oh shut up, you ridiculous little tosser," Ross said with a smile. There was a knock on the door, and he went to answer it. When he came back a few moments later, he had Lily with him. Kris sat up completely and got to his feet.

"Lily," He said, she greeted him with a hug, "are you alright?"

"Yes," she said, "I'm just fine. I'm just coming to see how you two are."

"Us?" Ross said, "yes, we're just fine and dandy."

"That's good," Lily said.

"Would you like to sit down for a moment?" Kris asked her.

"Yes, I think so," She went over and sat down on the sofa, and Kris went over and sat beside her. Ross took over the recliner. She looked over and seemed to notice Kris's suit, "you look nice today."

"Had to go to a funeral today," he said.

"My condolences."

"I was mostly there to be a shoulder for Zeke to cry on."

"Ah yes," Lily said, "his sister, right?"

Kris nodded. "So how are you doing?" Kris asked, "And how is your lovely fiancé?"

"Alexander and I are just fine. We're getting everything ready for the wedding in a couple of weeks. It'll be an outdoor wedding. Hopefully, the weather will cooperate, then again, after today's Spring rain, I don't know if I can trust it."

"A couple of weeks," Kris said.

"Will you be coming to the wedding?" She looked into his eyes expectantly, "both of you are welcome."

"You know, I don't know if that would be a good idea," Kris said, "but I am happy for both of you. We'll be sure and send a gift."

"I see," she said, "you'll both be missed. Well, I just stopped by to see how you both were. It seems that you're both on the mend."

"Oh yeah," Ross said, "dragons heal fast."

"I know," Lily said. She got to her feet, as did Kris. She hugged him. "Take care of yourself, alright?"

"Not to worry," Kris said, "we're tough bastards."

"You are," she said. He walked her to the door and opened it.

"Congratulations," he said, "I'm happy for you."

"Thank you," she said, "I'll be seeing you, Kris. Bye for now."

Then she was gone, and Kris came back to his chair and his beer. He put his feet up again. Ross sat down in his place on the sofa. "You really liked her, didn't you?"

"Yes, I did," Kris said, "but you and I are together, and she's got her own love."

"You love me?" Ross smiled.

"Yes, I love you. I've always loved you. I think it's that fucking bit of soul poking through again."

"I like that bit of soul."

"I find it exasperating."

"Yeah, I can understand that. And in case you're wondering, I love you too."

Kris scowled, "well yeah you do! How could you resist, dumbass?"

"You're right, I couldn't," Ross got up and walked over to where Kris sat and bent over him, placing a soft kiss upon his lips.

Kris smiled up at him, "you're such a sweet fucking lover."

They both laughed. This was going to be just fine. Kris was happy with this.

***

Zeke didn't like the fact that the MLD had basically turned him into a delivery boy. When they had discovered that he was returning to England, they had decided that they weren't going to just let him go. If he was going to go, he had to take something with him. The object in question was a vampire. It wasn't Charles. He had already been sent. The one he was being forced to transport was the woman Sandra. She still lived. He was taking her to her execution over there. He didn't really want to, but they needed someone, and they had set him up with a private plane, so why not? He just had to make sure that she was delivered to the MLA, the Magical Laws Agency.

When he boarded the plane at the airport, she was already there, basically wrapped in chains in one of the seats. He could smell the scent of dead blood on her. It was probably the only thing keeping her from breaking loose. He put his bag in one of the overhead bins and then sat down in one of the seats across from the woman as the one flight attendant went about her work and the pilot got ready for takeoff. He just sat there for a moment, watching her. She didn't speak to him or even acknowledge him at all. She was expressionless.

The plane finally took off. Zeke tried to ignore his traveling companion, but she was staring at him with expressionless eyes. It was really creeping him out. He couldn't help himself. He had to try and speak to her. "Are you in there?" He asked.

She looked up at him, into his eyes. She glared at him. It was the first inkling of any life or emotion from her, "what do you think?"

"I was just checking," he said, "you were giving me dead fish eyes."

"Dead man's blood has that effect on our kind."

"You're the one who shot Kris, aren't you?" He asked.

"Yes, I am. But don't worry. His dragon whore got me good for hurting him," she smiled at him.

"Why did you do this? I mean, what were you getting out of your dealings with Charles? Was it money?"

"Yes and no," she said, "In all truth, I didn't have much of a choice," she said, "I owed him in ways that you wouldn't understand. However, saying that I didn't have a choice wouldn't matter. I still get to die for his crimes."

Zeke shook his head in confusion, "you're right, I don't understand. What exactly did you owe him? What was he holding over you?"

"Does it really matter now?" She asked, "I am going to my death, regardless of whether or not anyone understands why. The question means nothing. It won't change anything."

"You never know, it might. I mean, if a feren were to search your mind..."

"They won't find it. They could scour my mind a million times over and never find it because it's shielded."

"Shielded?" Zeke had never heard of that before, "what do you mean, shielded?"

"Exactly what I said. That part of my mind had been shielded using powerful magic. Charles knew witches who could do that sort of thing."

"You'd rather die than reveal a secret that might save your life?"

"It wouldn't save me," she gave an annoyed snort, "you know nothing."

"I know nothing? Have it your own way then. I don't care if you're going to choose not to fight for yourself."

"Why would you even care?" She asked, "I almost killed your friend a couple of times. The dragon had to torture me to get information out of me. No, I'm not telling anyone anything if I don't have to. Just let me die, you dick."

"Fine," he said, "I don't care."

"It sounded like you did."

"Well, I don't."

"Whatever," she said, "just shut the fuck up."

He could definitely do that. He didn't give a shit about her, especially if she wasn't going to try and save herself. He was pretty sure that the MLA might spare her if they felt that she was doing things against her will. It didn't matter. He wanted to think about what he was going to do when he got there. He had friends that he needed to go see and places to visit. He didn't want to be bothered by annoying people who wouldn't help themselves.

"I hated him," she said, "so much, but I had no choice."

"What?" He asked, "I thought you didn't want to talk to me."

"Maybe I changed my mind," she said, "It's ancient magic that he used to bind me to him. It creates vampire slaves that must do as they're told. They *must* do what they are told."

"I have never heard of that before," Zeke said.

"Then what, it doesn't exist?" She rolled her eyes.

"I didn't say that," he said, "he didn't take advantage of you..."

"Not like that. He made me kill for him, that's it."

"My God," he said, "you have to tell them about this." His mind couldn't help but wonder what might have happened to Kris. Charles had made him. Would he have enslaved him like that?

"It probably still won't change anything," she said.

"It might not," he said, "it might change everything."

"I don't know about that."

"What if there are other vampires under similar spells? You could help them. You could save them from the pain that you experienced."

"I suppose you're right."

"Thank you for telling me," he said, "you certainly didn't have to."

"I know," she said.

"It'll be okay, I think. If you just tell them what you told me, then I think you'll be alright."

After that, she went quiet again. She was resting. The poison was difficult on her as it was on all vampires. He had to help her. He didn't know why he felt he had to help her, but he did, and he would. His thoughts returned to Kris. His friend had probably escaped a fate worse than death. He needed to know what this magic was so that he could stop it. If it were the work of witches, then they would have to be dealt with. He couldn't let others of his kind suffer as she had. Whatever she had done for him, if it was indeed against her will, then this magic could not be allowed to be used ever again. He wasn't officially a part of the MLD, or any magical law enforcement agency. However, he felt like he had a responsibility now. If it were true. There were ways to test for magic upon people. If she were lying to him, he would be very, very angry. If there was one thing that Zeke hated, it was being fooled.

CHAPTER 31

Two months later, Ross and Kris had both gone back to work. Kris was investigating another murder, a vampire who had actually murdered someone. It was pretty straight forward, and he was really bored. Then the Feren Lydia Danse came to his desk. She laid a file down on his desk.

He opened the file and saw the face of a little girl with dark hair and sad blue eyes, "what's this?"

"This little girl went missing three weeks ago in Portland, Oregon. This morning she was found here in Calgary. Her "parents" brought her into the MLD because she killed their neighbor."

"She's one of the trafficked children?" Kris asked.

"Yes, I'm taking her home to Oregon, and I was wondering if you would come with me and help me find Anderson's associates in Portland."

"I would like to, but I have to talk to my boyfriend before I make that type of decision."

"I understand," Lydia said, "We'll be heading back tomorrow."

"That's really short notice."

"Yes, I know, but I really need to get back."

"Alright," he said, "I'll call you after I talk to him."

"Wonderful. I hope you can come," she said. She walked away, and Kris went back to his work.

That night, he sat across from Ross at the dinner table. Kris didn't really eat, but he kind of liked watching Ross eat raw meat right in front of him. Blood dripped from his mouth as he chomped on the ribs. "Enjoying your meal?" Kris asked, watching the blood running down Ross's chin.

"Very much so," Ross said through bites of the meat. "I heard you got a visitor today."

"It was Lydia Danse," Kris sipped from a wine glass of blood, "she wants me to go with her to Portland, Oregon to try and bring down the vampire child traffickers."

"And you want to do that?"

"I don't know..."

"You feel you have to?"

"I do. This is one of Charles's wrongs that I can help right. I would kind of like to try."

"It could be dangerous, and you don't have any friends there."

"I know."

"But if you feel like you should..."

"I do."

"Then you should go."

Kris downed the rest of his blood, "but before I do, you want to go have some crazy sex?"

"That sounds wonderful," Ross got up, "just let me get cleaned up."

"No," Kris said, "Don't get cleaned up. Let's make a fucking mess." Kris got up and kissed Ross hard on the mouth. The next morning, Ross was trying to treat all the stains in the sheets as Kris packed his bag to leave. He could hear Ross swearing in the kitchen. Kris laughed to himself, *those fucking stains are never going to come out.*

EPILOGUE

Soon after arriving in Portland

Kris sat in the back of his cage. He had been in his steel barred prison for at least a week, and he was once again pumped full of the poison he hated so much. He didn't know who these people were, or what they wanted. All he knew was that they knew what he was, and that wasn't good. He was in what appeared to be an old barn. From what he could tell from the sounds he could hear nearby; it was at the actual ass end of nowhere. There were no sounds of cars, or people, or anything. He did hear a cow moo every so often, but that was about it. His captors hadn't hurt him, but they weren't going to let him go either.

He paced back and forth behind the bars. He hoped that the Magical Investigative Services had informed the MLD that he was missing. Ross would be here in a second. He looked up at a black object on the wall that he had decided was a camera. He casually flipped it off. Whoever these assholes were, they did not deserve any of his respect. *Fucking assholes...*

Other titles by **BLKDOG** Publishing that you might enjoy.

The Ring
By Sarah Anne Carter

A story of love, loss and hope.

Amanda knows three things about her life – she loves living in Tacoma, she wants to be a teacher and she will never marry a man in the military. Yet, when Lucas comes into the coffee shop where she works wearing a flight suit, he starts to change her mind about her future. She is determined to just be his friend, but the chemistry between them in undeniable and their relationship survives through two deployments and him being on work trips almost half of the time.

After they get married, they move across the country to Charleston, S.C., and Amanda finds a job, which helps somewhat with the loneliness of Lucas being gone a lot. She thought she was prepared for life as a military wife, but then she starts finding out the true sacrifices military families make.

Arthur: Shadow of a God
By Richard Denham

King Arthur has fascinated the Western world for over a thousand years and yet we still know nothing more about him now than we did then. Layer upon layer of heroics and exploits has been piled upon him to the point where history, legend, and myth have become hopelessly entangled.

In recent years, there has been a sort of scholarly consensus that 'the once and future king' was clearly some sort of Romano-British warlord, heroically stemming the tide of wave after wave of Saxon invaders after the end of Roman rule. But surprisingly, and no matter how much we enjoy this narrative, there is actually next-to-nothing solid to support this theory except the wishful thinking of understandably bitter contemporaries. The sources and scholarship used to support the 'real Arthur' are as much tentative guesswork and pushing 'evidence' to the extreme to fit in with this version as anything involving magic swords, wizards and dragons. Even Archaeology remains silent. Arthur is, and always has been, the square peg that refuses to fit neatly into the historians round hole.

Arthur: Shadow of a God gives a fascinating overview of Britain's lost hero and casts a light over an often-overlooked and somewhat inconvenient truth; Arthur was almost certainly not a man at all, but a god. He is linked inextricably to the world of Celtic folklore and Druidic traditions. Whereas tyrants like Nero and Caligula were men who fancied themselves gods; is it not possible that Arthur was a god we have turned into a man? Perhaps then there is a truth here. Arthur, 'The King under the Mountain'; sleeping until his return will never return, after all, because he doesn't need to. Arthur the god never left in the first place and remains as popular today as he ever was. His legend echoes in stories, films, and games that are every bit as imaginative and fanciful as that which the minds of talented bards such as Taliesin and Aneirin came up with when the mists of the 'dark ages' still swirled over Britain – and perhaps that is a good thing after all, most at home in the imaginations of children and adults alike – being the Arthur his believers want him to be.

A Storm of Magic
By Ashley Laino

Being brought back from the dead is an impressive trick, even for magician Darien Burron. Now he must try and use his sleight of hand to swindle modern-day witch, Mirah, to sign her power away, or end up a tormented demon in the afterlife.

Meanwhile, sixteen-year-old Mirah is starting to lose control of her powers. After an incident at her aunt's Witchery store, Mirah is sent to a secret coven to learn to control her abilities. While away, Mirah meets up with a soft-spoken clairvoyant, a brazen storm witch, and the creator of dark magic itself. The young woman must learn to trust in herself before she loses herself entirely to the darkness that hunts her.

Weirder War Two
By Richard Denham & Michael Jecks

Did a Warner Bros. cartoon prophesize the use of the atom bomb? Did the Allies really plan to use stink bombs on the enemy? Why did the Nazis make their own version of Titanic and why were polar bear photographs appearing throughout Europe?

The Second World War was the bloodiest of all wars. Mass armies of men trudged, flew or rode from battlefields as far away as North Africa to central Europe, from India to Burma, from the Philippines to the borders of Japan. It saw the first aircraft carrier sea battle and the indiscriminate use of terror against civilian populations in ways not seen since the Thirty Years War. Nuclear and incendiary bombs erased entire cities. V weapons brought new horror from the skies: the V1 with their hideous grumbling engines, the V2 with sudden, unexpected death. People were systematically starved: in Britain food had to be rationed because of the stranglehold of U-Boats, while in Holland the German blockade of food and fuel saw 30,000 die of starvation in the winter of 1944/5. It was a catastrophe for millions.

At a time of such an enormous crisis, scientists sought ever more inventive weapons, or devices to help halt the war. Civilians were involved as never before, with women taking up new trades, proving themselves as capable as their male predecessors whether in the factories or the fields.

The stories in this book are of courage, of ingenuity, of hilarity in some cases, or of great sadness, but they are all thought-provoking - and rather weird. So whether you are interested in the last Polish cavalry charge, the Blackout Ripper, Dada, or Ghandi's attempt to stop the bloodshed, welcome to the Weirder War Two!

Click Bait
By Gillian Philip

A funny joke's a funny joke. Eddie Doolan doesn't think twice about adapting it to fit a tragic local news story and posting it on social media.

It's less of a joke when his drunken post goes viral. It stops being funny altogether when Eddie ends up jobless, friendless and ostracised by the whole town of Langburn. This isn't how he wanted to achieve fame.

Eddie knows he's blown his relationship with rich girl Lily Cumnock. It's Lily's possessive and controlling father Brodie who fires him from his job - and makes sure he won't find another decent one in Langburn. And Eddie doesn't even have Flo to fall back on - his old nan died some six months ago, and Eddie is still recovering from the death of the woman who raised him and who loved him unconditionally.

Under siege from the press, and facing charges not just for the joke but for a history of abusive behaviour on the internet, Eddie grows increasingly paranoid and desperate. The only people still speaking to him are Crow, a neglected kid who relies on Eddie for food and company, and Sid, the local gamekeeper's granddaughter. It's Sid who offers Eddie a refuge and an understanding ear.

But she also offers him an illegal shotgun - and as Eddie's life spirals downwards, and his efforts at redemption are thwarted at every turn, the gun starts to look like the answer to all his problems.

Burning Bridges
By Chris Bedell

They've always said that three's a crowd...

24-year-old Sasha didn't anticipate her identical twin Riley killing herself upon their reconciliation after years of estrangement. But Sasha senses an opportunity and assumes Riley's identity so she can escape her old life.

Playing Riley isn't without complications, though. Riley's had a strained relationship with her wife and stepson so Sasha must do whatever she can to make her newfound family love and accept her. If Sasha's arrangement ends, then she'll have nothing protecting her from her past. However, when one of Sasha's former clients tracks her down, Sasha must choose between her new life and the only person who cared about her.

But things are about to become even more complicated, as a third sister, Katrina, enters the scene...

**Father of Storms
By Dean Jones**

Imagine losing everything you loved as well as the future you'd wished for so long to come true.

Seth was born with the gift to manipulate energy, unfortunately, his skills mark him as a target for one who wishes to control everything. So began a life running from those who would seek to command him, a life that spans over a thousand years waiting for the day when all will be once again as it was. Captured in modern day London, Seth needs the help of his companions, the Mara, to show him who he is through dreams of his past, so he can save the family he has waited so long to have.

A warrior bred for battle must fight once more but this time the battlefield is his mind. Can Seth win, or will he finally lose who he is and become the weapon of the man who started his nightmare all those years ago?
Father of Storms is a story told through time, a tale of love and hope where there seems to be none and above all, it is a reminder that if you believe, truly believe then even from the darkest places, good things come to those who wait.

www.blkdogpublishing.com

www.ingramcontent.com/pod-product-compliance
Lightning Source LLC
Chambersburg PA
CBHW011921050726
47591CB00007B/2284